THE MAGIC CUPCAKE

RIVER LAURENT

The Magic Cupcake

ISBN: ISBN: 978-1-911608-27-1

Chapter One

LAUREN

"Have you ever had a day when EVERYTHING went wrong?"

I open my eyes on Friday the 16th thinking it is going to be the best day of my life. Outside, the sun is shining brightly and I just know I'm going to kill it at the big presentation I'll be making later. It is the most important and biggest milestone of my career, but I am so prepared and ready my body feels like it is vibrating. I spring out of bed so fast I startle Draco, who gives a little yelp of surprise.

On my way to the kitchen, the doorbell rings.

There is a big smile on my face as I open the door to the postman. "Good morning, Tom," I greet him brightly.

"I see someone's in a good mood this morning," he remarks handing me a package.

It's not for me, it's for my roomie, Danny. While I'm signing for it, Draco makes a mad dash for the door.

"Come back here," I yell.

Of course, he doesn't come back. Ducking through the gap, he runs to my super sexy, emerald-eyed, completely lickable neighbor's front door. Calmly, he does his morning business on the brown welcome mat.

"No, Draco, no!"

Normally, such behavior from Draco would have annoyed me, but not this morning. This morning, I'm on fire. The poo is a dry, well-formed thing so cleaning it up should be fairly easy. No one needs to know, especially not my hot neighbor.

The man moved in two weeks ago and I guess I have a bit of crush on him. Who wouldn't? The man looks like he stepped out of an Abercrombie and Fitch life size poster. He's the first man I can imagine pouring cream on his abs and licking it all off.

I rush off to the kitchen, get some cleaning supplies, and hurry out again, only to see Mr. Abercrombie open his front door and step right into Draco's shit. All my fantasies of putting on a coat of raspberry lipstick and my long black dress before knocking on his door to borrow a cup of sugar evaporate into nothing right before my eyes.

His gaze moves from the mess under his shoe and starts travelling upwards. Slowly. From my fluffy bear slippers, up my stripy pajamas, to my hands clutching paper towels and cleaning liquid, higher up to my chest, then the tips of my sleep-tangled hair, then on to my neck and unmade face. He stops at my frankly horrified eyes.

For a second, neither of us moves.

We just stare at each other. God, the guy has a really sensuous mouth. And that lantern jaw. You could start a war with it.

"Hi," I whisper. Surprisingly, my voice comes out sounding all hoarse and sexy. This might work out after all. Draco's talent might have been matchmaker all along. In fact, this could be the beginning of a totally awesome romance.

But he doesn't return the greeting, he exhales emitting a short, disbelieving sound. There is a flicker of something in his eyes. Looks a bit like annoyance or irritation.

I blink and wake up from my ridiculous fantasy. *What the hell are you doing staring at him like a love-struck teenager?* Without thinking, I rush forward suddenly, and crouching in front of him, start cleaning his shoe with the paper towels while apologizing frantically. I can hear myself…I sound like a demented pigeon, but I can't stop.

"Leave it. It's fine," he says.

But he has one of those panty-melting voices that confuses me and makes me grab onto the hard muscles of his calf as I double down on my task of getting rid of the poo. Somehow, I manage to lift his shoe off the mat and finish the task. "There you go. All done," I say, lifting my head. I am now eye-level with his crotch. Holy Moly! It looks like he's packing a seriously big lunchbox in there.

At this point, my neighbor abruptly steps away from me.

Hot blood floods into my face as I stand up. I can't believe I was staring at his crotch. I can't even look him in the eye. What an idiot I am.

"Well, thank you for that," he says suavely.

"Don't worry. I'll—I'll get the mat cleaned o-off," I stutter.

"No need. I'll get another one."

I shake my head. "No, no, I absolutely insist."

He frowns, then nods his utterly gorgeous head, and walks off.

"Stupid, stupid, stupid," I curse myself, watching from the window at the end of the hall as his olive-green Maserati roars off. I pick his mat up by the edge. What is the matter with me? Why on earth did I not just say that I would replace the mat?

It takes ages for me to hose down the damn thing. And the smell! Draco can make glass melt with some of his messes and this one is no exception. It puts me right off breakfast. Funny though, how I didn't even notice it while I was crouched in front of that man's lovely thighs.

I put it all behind me while I'm in the shower. I need to focus on looking my best. I get into the clothes I have already laid out last night and carefully do my face and hair. Slipping into my lucky shoes, I take a deep breath and go to stand in front of the full-length mirror in the hallway. Yes, I look the part. My shoulders are straight, and I'm fully determined to put the morning's incident, well, all right—humiliating fiasco, behind me and take on the world.

"Wish me luck, Draco," I whisper in his ear.

He tries to turn his head and slobber all over my face, but I'm too quick for him.

"Nah, you've done enough damage this morning, don't you think?"

He makes a disapproving noise as I close the front door. I walk to the parking lot and slide behind the wheel of my car, turn on the ignition, and the damn thing won't start. But it worked fine last night.

Calm down, Lauren. Calm down. You still have plenty of time.

Chapter Two

LAUREN

As Danny is away on holiday, I can't even get him to drop me off. Not wanting to be late on such an important day, I call a taxi even though it is going to cost the earth. The driver drops me off at the end of the block because he wants to avoid the traffic coming down the road. It's only a fifty-yard walk, but then just outside the entrance of my office building, the right heel of my shoes gets stuck in one of the cracks in the sidewalk.

Damn!

I try to pull it out and it breaks off. There is no way I'm leaving the heel in the crack because these are my lucky shoes and I need luck today. Cursing and swearing, I pull the heel out and hobble to my office. Jenny, our receptionist produces a tube of glue which she says is similar to Gorilla glue. I've used Gorilla glue before and that stuff is amazing. I look at the label and it says strong as nails. While I am holding the two pieces together, Jenny reveals that she bought the glue at the dollar shop. I ignore the twinge of anxiety.

Of course, half-way through my presentation, and I'm

doing brilliantly too, my heel, well…falls off with a quiet thud.

There's a whole room of silent people watching me with bated breath so I get the brilliant idea to rise above the situation by making my predicament into a joke.

"Who needs shoes, anyway?" I quip as I take off my shoes and throw them up into the air. The first one lands on the table making a couple of people jump, and the second one bounces off the wall and strikes the boss of the company we are presenting to right in the face.

Everyone freezes in horror and I stare at Mr. Montfort in disbelief. This cannot be happening to me. No way.

People stand up and start moving towards him. There are offers to get him ice and generally help him. I don't know whether he is a sadist, or a masochist, but with a stony expression, he insists I carry on with my presentation.

Trying to impress someone whose face is slowly swelling up and turning blue-black is not an easy thing to do. It's not surprising that I make a complete cock-up of my carefully rehearsed spiel. Avoiding the eyes of the rest of my horrified team, I stumble, stutter, and mumble my way to the last slide.

"Well, that's it. As you can see, you can't possibly go wrong by choosing our company," I conclude with a bright smile. But it is so fake even a two-month old baby would have seen through it.

When we leave, our competitors, who are waiting outside, can't stop smirking. They can tell by the expressions on our faces we have had a disaster. I try to walk with my head held high, but as the elevator doors close behind my team and me, they all turn on me furiously.

"What the fuck was that all about?"

"How could you, Lauren?"

"Christ, do you even realize what you've just done?"

"Are you really that stupid?"

Hell, I hardly recognize them. They're like venomous snakes in a pit. Hissing and spitting at me, but I can't blame them. I'd feel the same if one of them had done this to me. This is a big deal for my company, for all of us. We've been working day and night for seven months solid and I guess we all counted our chickens before the eggs were even laid. We couldn't help it; our product and system was just that much better than all our competitors!

I apologize profusely, but it doesn't make any difference. I have smashed all their hopes.

When I get back to the office, I'm called to go face my boss. Haltingly, I explain what happened. I have never seen my boss turn white before and I'm sorry to be the one who did that to him. He's a nice guy and I really like him. I know he was really counting on this deal to take our company to the next level.

"I mean, we could still win the contract. Our proposal is solid," I mumble unconvincingly.

He drops his face into his palms.

I sneak out when he starts making strange sobbing noises behind his hands. I figure he needs some privacy.

As if that is not enough, my mother calls in tears because my sister has agreed to marry her unemployed, good-for–nothing, lay-about boyfriend. Since I'm so toxic around the office, no one even wants to make eye contact, I let my mother persuade me to go around to my sister's place so I could help persuade her that she's making a mistake.

Another bad mistake on my part.

I get stuck for an hour listening to Christine describe how terribly misunderstood her boyfriend is, and how wonderful he really is. The way she describes him, he is Mother Theresa with a dick. While she's talking, I keep seeing my shoe bounce off the wall in slow motion, hitting Mr. Montfort in the face. In the end, I have no choice but to force myself to agree with my sister that her boyfriend is indeed awesome, just so I can escape the relentless monologue.

I get out on the street and feel like shit. The shock is wearing off and I know I have messed up big time. I've ruined it for everyone else as well. Everyone is angry with me, but it's not completely my fault. I'm the victim not the villain. I wanted that proposal as much as anyone else.

As I'm standing there wanting to burst into tears, Andrea, one of my two best friends calls.

"Hey, you. How did it go?" she asks.

"Don't ask. I so freaking bombed," I mutter.

"Oh, that bad? Does that mean the big office celebration is off?"

"Maybe they're all going, but I don't think I would be welcome. They'll probably make a voodoo doll of my likeness and take turns stabbing pins into it."

"You sure you don't want to talk about it?"

"Not yet."

"Right," she says crisply. "You need to relax, my child. We're meeting at the Green Man. Six-thirty, okay with you?"

My chin wobbles slightly. "I don't think I'm going to be good company."

"You can't be worse than you usually are," she says cheerfully.

"It's not funny, Andrea. I feel really horrible. I totally screwed up the presentation."

"No way. You could have recited that in your sleep."

"I threw my shoe at Mr. Montfort," I wail miserably."

"What?"

"See the problem now?"

For a second there is silence. Then she clears her throat. "Look, let's get this into perspective. Did you drop a bomb on an innocent population of people?"

"No."

"Okay. Did you invent a hazardous bio-weapon capable of killing millions, and then sell the formula to a couple of bad guys?"

"Obviously not."

"Then, chin up. Every cloud has a silver lining."

"Not this one," I mutter.

"Please don't be late."

"I don't know, Andrea…"

"Just remember if you don't come, we'll both turn up at your place and we'll stay the night," she warns before the line goes dead.

For a second, I stand on the sidewalk, undecided. I guess I could go and have one drink. It's been a horrible day, and I richly deserve one drink after the day I've had. I call Mira, my dog walker and arrange for her to take Draco out for his evening walk, then I hail a taxi.

Of course, to top the day off, I get stuck in a terrible traffic jam and end up having to walk half the way. By the time I open the door of the bar, I have determined I'm going to finish the day in a spectacular way. I'm going to get wasted in a way I've never ever allowed myself to get.

Glancing around the crowded bar, it's not hard to spot my friends.

Andrea, with her white-blond bob, tall and elegant, propped up against the bar. She's rolling her eyes and smirking.

Nina, all curvy and vivacious in her fitting red suit is gesturing wildly with her hands. Model-gorgeous, she's easily my most beautiful friend, by far. And she has a string of brokenhearted ex-boyfriends to prove it.

Bless their sweet souls, there are three dirty martinis lined up between them. They are all mine. God, I'm so glad I decided not to stay at home on my own and joined these two brilliant girls instead.

"Lauren!" they both chime and pull me into a hug.

"We ordered you your usual," Nina says, handing me a martini glass.

Oh, yes! We clink, and before they can toast to the weekend the way we normally do, I suck down half the glass in one swig. It goes down so briny, smooth, and cold it almost makes me forget Mr. Montfort's stunned expression. I close my eyes to truly appreciate the blessing.

"You had that coming for sure," Nina declares, patting my arm. She tilts her head so her dark curls spill all over her shoulder and looks at me strangely. Andrea would have told her about me attacking Mr. Montfort.

"Damn straight. I've been waiting for this all day without knowing it." I finish the glass and thump it down on the bar. I should go easy. I missed breakfast and only managed to find time to stuff down a blueberry muffin before going to meet my blazing ball of humiliation. Of course, after Mr. Montfort's unfortunate encounter with my shoe… I completely lost my appetite and haven't eaten anything else.

"I've been counting the minutes till you got here," Andrea complains, rolling her eyes and jerking a thumb in Nina's direction. "This one's been bragging about how big Ryan's dick is."

I almost spit out precious vodka at this. "Wow. Nobody likes a braggart." "What?" Nina's big blue eyes are all innocence. "Since when did telling the truth become bragging?"

An image of me crouching in front of my neighbor's crotch flashes into my mind and I want to cringe. Ugh. I put the picture out of my mind firmly. I'll deal with that later. Right now, I'm with my best friends and I'm not going to let anything get me down.

"Oh, please. You know very well, neither Lauren nor me have had any in forever and a week," Andrea scolds.

"Like you guys never talked about the size of the dicks you were riding, even when I wasn't getting any," she says sulkily.

"We talked. We did not brag." Andrea elbows her. "Big difference."

"Okay, I'm sorry, but there are just certain things that deserve to be talked about; Ryan's dick is one of them. There's practically two of them. It's that big."

"I hate you so much right now," I mutter, before starting on my last martini.

"I bought you all those drinks, girl," she informs me.

I raise my glass in a toast to her. "Thanks, babe. But you know what, I still hate you."

Nina laughs, and as the sound of her laughter washes over me, I'm already feeling better. I never feel better than I do when I'm hanging out with these two. I signal for one of the servers as we catch each other's eye from opposite ends of the long, polished bar because… *oh, look, I'm already empty.*

"So, you're feeling a little under-appreciated by the opposite sex, are you?" Nina shrugs like this is no problem at all—but then, it's never been one for her.

"That's an understatement," I say, thinking of my neighbor's quick escape from me this morning.

"Like the two of you couldn't easily pick up any man in this bar," Nina insists, waving her arms around and causing her bracelets to jangle together. "You're both hot and you know it." She turns to me. "Look at you. You're drop-dead gorgeous."

"Am I?"

"Of course you are," they both chorus at the same time.

The alcohol is starting to race around in my bloodstream, but even then, I know they're only saying this because they're my friends. And friends are supposed to say things like that to bolster each other's feelings, especially when they have just thrown a shoe in the face of the man they have been working seven months to impress. The fact is I'm pretty medium, all things considered. Medium height, brown hair, hazel eyes. Nothing special. Even my curves aren't all that curvy. Meanwhile, Nina's an Amazon and Andrea's got the body that makes men drool.

"There must be somebody you're interested in," Andrea wheedles.

"Not really."

"So why are you blushing?" Nina smiles coyly at me.

Chapter Three

LAUREN

My face feels like it is on fire. "Hmmm, no one realistically in my league. Just eye candy, you know," I try to say dismissively. "So what's this I hear about a promotion coming up for you anyway?"

Nina's eyes become huge. She leans forward. "Oh, don't think you're going to change the subject that easily. Tell us about him!"

"Yeah, it's been ages since you've even shown an interest in anyone," Andrea adds. "So even if he's just eye candy, we want all the details. Name? Address? Cock size? The works!"

I roll my eyes. Where do I start? I don't even know his name so it sounds ridiculous that I have a crush on this guy. "It's my neighbor. He moved in next door around two weeks ago."

Nina's perfectly-arched eyebrows wiggle up and down. "Ooh, the new next-door-neighbor! Intriguing."

"From two weeks ago?" Andrea asks impatiently.

"Yup."

"Well, what does he look like?" Nina asks.

"It doesn't matter. Trust me, it's a non-starter," I answer, suddenly feeling a little depressed. I signal the bartender for another drink. I'm going to need it if this is what the night is going to turn into.

"Why is it a non-starter?" Nina asks, pouncing on me.

"I think he hates me, if you must know. Which is why it's not even worth talking about him."

"I don't think it would be possible for anybody to hate you," Andrea says loyally.

"You're sweet, but you didn't look into his eyes." I just about want to slump over on the table with the memory.

"Is he good-looking?" Nina asks.

An image of my gorgeous neighbor randomly pops into my head and I feel my face getting hot. "I guess he is." It comes out in a breathless sigh and I feel like a teenage girl again. *Get a grip, Lauren!* I take a deep breath. "Yes, he's tall, dark, handsome, and mysterious, but I barely know anything about him, really!"

"So, why didn't you be a good neighbor and bake him some cakes or something?" Nina asks, incredulously. "That's what I would have done. And you make the best cupcakes! Is he definitely single? You should get in there quick before he gets snapped up. Or maybe he's single for a reason..." she trails off.

"Jeez, Nina, chill out," Andrea says, coming to my rescue. Or so I think... "Look, if you think he's really hot, why not at least try and chat to him for a bit next time you bump into him."

They're each as bad as the other, but I guess he *is* the first guy I've mentioned for a while. Since my last relationship ended more than two years ago. My stomach lurches involuntarily and I quickly put that thought to the back of my head. Of course, there is one little detail I've failed to tell them about my gorgeous neighbor...

"The thing is," I admit, "I was actually planning on introducing myself and everything."

"Yes?" Nina prompts.

"Yeah, well, if there was any chance of anything happening there, my little sweetheart ruined that this morning."

"Oh, no. What did he do?" Andrea asks, stricken. "He didn't bite him, did he?"

"You know he wouldn't do that." I roll my eyes, sighing heavily at the memory. "He ran out when the postman came by and decided to poop all over my neighbor's welcome mat. I mean, for a 12-pound Yorkie, that dog can seriously take a dump. I'm pretty sure he lost half his body weight on that mat."

"No!" Andrea bursts out laughing.

"Oh, bless him, poor Draco," Nina says sympathetically.

I adore her undying love and affection for my dear old dog. I hold my head in my hands. "Before I could run back inside to grab stuff to pick it up with, my neighbor opened his door and stepped right the hell into the middle of it."

"No…", both of them cry in unison.

"And he was wearing a really expensive pair of shoes too," I groan. "I wanted to die. And he looked at me like he wanted me to die too."

"Awkward!" Andrea laughs, who seems to be enjoying this far too much for my liking. "This is exactly the reason I refuse to have pets. So, what happened then?"

"Yeah, what happened then?" Nina probes, her eyes shining with curiosity and naughtiness.

"I did something really, really stupid."

"What?" both of them ask eagerly.

"I crouched in front of him and started cleaning his shoe."

Andrea's eyes widen with surprise. "Oh, you sly fox, you."

"It's not like what you think. He stepped away real fast." I smack my forehead. "God, I was so stupid. I've blown any chance I may have had, let's put it that way."

"Have you seen him since?" Nina asks, always the optimist.

"That was this morning," I reply glumly.

Nina slides an arm around my shoulders. "But hey, things like this happen. It's not the end of the world. And now you've at least broken the ice, right?"

"Sure, we've broken the ice. But I swear, he'll never talk to me again. You didn't see the way he looked at me, guys."

Nina pats me on the back. "Okay, so it won't work out between the two of you. No biggie. His loss. There are plenty of fish in the sea."

"Sure. I'll just have to keep seeing him around, every time we cross paths in the hall. I'll have to hear him in his apartment."

Andrea frowns, exchanging a glance with Nina. "You're really into him, aren't you?"

I shrug, trying to play it off, but I can't hold my disappointment in. "Yeah, I think I kind of built a fantasy around him. I know it's stupid, but he really is fantasy material. He's everything a girl dreams about. Tall and dark with broad shoulders and these green eyes…" I close my own eyes, remembering them. I remember the way they narrowed when he looked down and realized what he stepped in. What my dog did. Timing truly is everything.

"You know…" Nina swirls the wine in her glass with her lips pursed. "If you're really into this guy…" She pauses, her eyes flitting tantalizingly between Andrea and me.

"Out with it," Andrea says impatiently.

"Okay. I know it might sound ridiculous," she begins, holding up both hands. "But just set aside your judgment for a one second and consider a possibility that you might not usually entertain."

Andrea is looking suspicious by now.

"Go on," I urge.

"Hold your horses. I'm about to. One of the girls I work with swears it's all legit. Maybe a little weird-sounding, maybe a little strange too, but…"

"Wow, whatever it is, I can't wait to try it," I joke before polishing off my fourth martini. I'm well past the point of being pleasantly buzzed. I should probably order something to eat to soak up all the booze, but why would I want to ruin the good feeling?

"You're the worst at getting to the important part of a story," Andrea grumbles as she signals the bartender for more. Happy Hour prices only last but so long, after all.

"Because I know you're both going to laugh. But this coworker of mine, she swore it worked. She told me this crazy story about how she met the guy she's with now. At first, he didn't like her at all. But now he's completely smitten and she even saw a receipt for an engagement ring in his pocket!" She pauses for effect just as another round of cocktails arrive.

"Go on then," I say, rolling my eyes. "What's your friend's big secret, then?"

She takes a generous sip before continuing, "She went to…" Her eyes dart back and forth, as she leans in to whisper, "A gypsy."

"A what?" I burst out laughing. "Oh, come on."

"Are we even allowed to use that word anymore?" Andrea wonders aloud.

"That's what she called her, and that's what the woman

calls herself. I don't know. Anyway, she gives out love potions."

"Is there something besides wine in your glass?" I ask. "Because you just sounded like you went and lost it."

Andrea can't stop giggling. "You know you sound insane, right? Things like that don't happen in real life."

"Fine, fine. Don't believe me if it makes you feel better, but just hear me out, ok?" She shrugs it off. "This friend of mind said it worked. She was super into this guy who she had a crush on for ages, but he didn't even know she was alive. Then she was at party and someone told her about this gypsy woman who lives in the Mission. Apparently, this gypsy woman whose name is Madam Zelda…"

Andrea starts sniggering. "Madam Zelda? That's just ridiculous."

Nina ignores her. "Madam Zelda decides if the match is meant to be by asking questions and stuff. If she thinks the couple deserves each other, then she makes a special love potion to make it happen. So my friend went to this woman and got a love potion from her and boom…The rest, as they say, is history."

"What?" Andrea practically chokes on her drink. "You are joking, right?"

I, on the other hand, can't help being at least a little curious. "And it really worked?" I ask Nina. "He really fell in love with her? How did she give it to him?"

"She baked it into a cookie for him. He ate it. Went home then phoned her up the next day and asked her out."

"Wow," I whisper. Even though I'm no longer sober, I recognize it is a ridiculous story. Andrea's right…things like that don't happen in real life. And yet…"It works on anybody at all?" I ask, stirring my martini with the skewered olives.

Andrea's jaw just about hits the floor. "Are you honestly entertaining this absurd idea?"

"Now, now, I'm only asking." I pop the olive in my mouth and grin.

"Good, because it is the most outrageous thing I've ever heard," Andrea says firmly.

I look at Nina. "Well?"

She frowns. "I don't know, but the way I understood it, the gypsy only gives the potions to people who deserve it."

"You mean, the people who can afford it," Andrea mutters.

"No, I mean the ones who deserve it," Nina insists. "She listens to your story – you know, you have to tell her who it is you're in love with and all that – and she can tell from listening to you if you're sincere and if you're not going to, ya know, abuse the…umm…power."

By this stage, Andrea's not even bothering to hide her total derision. She's shaking with uncontrollable laughter.

But I'm not. I'm intrigued. I can't help it. Maybe it's the booze. It's probably the booze. And the fact that I've only eaten vodka-soaked olives in the last seven hours. And the small problem that I haven't gotten laid in— Jesus, I've lost track of how long it's been. And the crazy way my heart jumps when I think of my neighbor. Besides, after the day I've had I deserve this. Whatever this is.

"So, do you want the number then?" she asks me, smiling.

"Wait a minute," Andrea butts in. "How come *you* have the gypsy's number? Have you spoken to her yourself?"

"Maybe…" she replies looking a little coy.

"Did you call her?" I ask. "About this guy you're seeing at the moment?"

She looks down and then nods. "Yeah, I did," she

admits, sighing dramatically. "But it turns out there's not a potion that will fix large penises."

"Did you seriously ask her that?" Andrea cries out, before breaking into a fit of laughter.

Nina sniffs. "Go ahead and laugh, but you don't know what it's like to try and stuff twelve inches inside you."

Andrea laughs so hard she starts gasping for breath. "Oh my god, I wish I could have listened to that conversation!"

I think of my neighbor's green eyes. For that one instant when our eyes first met and we had both stared at each other, I'd felt as if the rest of the world had fallen away, so there was only him and me. There had been something there. "Yes, I do want the number," I blurt out suddenly.

Andrea stops laughing and whirls her head around in my direction so fast I'm astonished she doesn't give herself a whiplash. "You've got to be kidding." She stares at me, then at Nina. "Did I just slip into some alternate reality here? First, Nina is asking a gypsy what she can do with a foot-long penis and now you want a love potion for your neighbor?" She shakes her head in disbelief. "You're honestly considering going through with this craziness?"

"There's no harm in trying."

"Except to your bank account. I'm sure this woman doesn't give away love potions out of the goodness of her heart. I'm sure they aren't free."

"It's my money," I remind her. She's a great friend and I love her dearly, but she's also a little bossy. Even more so when she's had a few glasses of alcohol. "All I want is a nice regular guy with no weird habits or interests, and a nice cock. Is that too much to ask?"

Andrea glares at Nina who looks back defiantly. "Would you please stop encouraging her? Can't you get your kicks from playing with a big, giant dick instead of getting her all riled up for your amusement?"

Nina holds her palms up. "Calm down. I'm just trying to help. She's an adult, you know. She can make up her own mind."

Andrea turns back to me. "Don't do it, babe," she begs. "Please."

I shrug carelessly. "After the kind of day I've had what harm can it possibly do?"

"After the day you've had is exactly why you shouldn't do it. You're not thinking straight and you've had all those martinis on an empty stomach, haven't you? Come on, Lauren. I promise you, you'll regret it in the morning. I can't let you blow your money when you're in this state."

My shoulders slump. "Do you guys know I've haven't even been out on a date for nearly two years because I wanted to focus on my career, but after what happened today not only can I forget any kind of promotion, I'm probably even out of a job."

They are both staring at me with pity in their eyes.

"I've been playing it safe and missed out on life all this while and for what? For fuck all." I can feel my voice slurring. "Plus…plus…I'll have to move out of my home now because I can't afford to keep paying rent on that place. Let me end this horrible day with a big bang, okay? I want to do something so crazy and insensible I can laugh about it when I am old and gray while sitting alone in a nursing home."

"All right, if you insist," Andrea gives in.

Nina grins victoriously as she opens her purse and fishes out her phone. She scrolls through it. "Here we go. *The* number."

Chapter Four

LAUREN

I don't know if it's the alcohol but I'm feeling extraordinarily excited about the whole thing. It's like an adventure. And I can't remember the last time I had an adventure. I think it was when I was a kid and my parents took me to a fun fair and I got lost in the Horror house. I was so terrified I nearly peed myself while I was inside, but when I got out at the other end, I felt very proud of myself.

I've never met a gypsy before or had my fortune told. In fact, I haven't done very much with my life at all. At the very least, this will be a new experience for me. I avoid making eye contact with Andrea's gaze as I find my own phone. The numbers of the screen look kinda blurry.

Fortunately, Nina gently relieves me of my phone and types the number into it for me.

I take my phone and clear my throat.

All I have to do is go through with the call. It's a little loud, here in the bar, but I can always go outside. I want to do this, I really want to, but my nerves are jangling like crazy the closer I come to going through with the craziest thing I've ever done. It's one thing to talk a big game, especially with Andrea telling me how nuts I am, but another to follow through.

"Shall I call her now?"

"Unless you need a little more liquid courage to go through with this?" Nina offers.

"I might. I might need a bit more."

"No, you don't," Andrea cuts in. "We'll both follow you out while you make your call."

I try to protest, but Andrea will not hear of it.

So we troop outside together. It's cold out. I use that as an excuse to huddle a little, my coat collar pulled up to sort of hide my face from my friends. At least the freezing air gives me a reason to have flushed cheeks.

It rings once…twice…maybe she won't pick up? I feel a sense of disappointment. What did I expect? This day is going to suck to the very end.

"Hello?"

I'm so startled I jump. The woman's voice is low, smoky. Dare I say exactly what I would've expected from a woman who sells love potions? I imagine her sitting in a dark room, wearing multiple layers of flowy, gauzy caftans or something, with a cigarette in a long holder sitting between her first two fingers. I've watched a lot of TV. Maybe too much. "Uh, is this Madam Zelda?"

"Yes," she says shortly.

I blink hard. "My name is Lauren." Andrea snorts loudly and I quickly turn my back to her. "I understand you provide—um—solutions to women."

"I provide many services to many young women. And the occasional young man. What is it you are looking for Zelda to provide?"

Talks about herself in third person. That's healthy. But then again, this could all be an act. She's got to keep up appearances. I clear my throat, ready to choke on the words, then cup my hand around my mouth before replying, "A-a—potion." Jesus, this is so weird.

"If you are calling at this time of the night it must be a love potion you are looking for."

"Yes, it's for love," I confirm, my stomach is a mess of nerves and excitement.

"I can certainly provide a love portion," she says in that smoky voice. "But it must be done tonight. There is a full moon. Come to my home no later than midnight, or it will be too late and I will see if I can help.

"You want me to come tonight?" I ask, throwing a panicked look at my friends.

Andrea shakes her head. "Tell her tomorrow," she mimes.

I turn away. "So you need the full moon to make your potion?"

"Yes, for it to work fully, a full moon is necessary."

I take a deep breath. "Alright, I'll come now."

"Us," Andrea hisses. "We are all going. I'm not letting you go to a stranger's house alone in the state you're in."

"Your friend is right," Zelda agrees.

My eyes widen. I had no idea she could hear that…or was she able to sense it? No. That would be ridiculous. I should've stopped at the third martini.

"So long as," she continues, "they respect the nature of the work which you and I will do together, your friends are welcome if you would feel more at ease with them in your presence."

"Yes, yes, I believe I would," I say in a rush, very glad I won't have to face the strange old gypsy woman myself.

"Wonderful. Bring four hundred dollars to the following address—"

"Four hundred?" I repeat stunned as I lock eyes with

Nina, who shrugs. I don't know why I was thinking it would be in the region of twenty dollars. I guess it's because in all the movies I've seen gypsies tell fortunes in exchange for tiny amounts of cash. I don't even dare look at Andrea. I know exactly what she's thinking.

"You want a love potion, do you not?" Zelda demands.

"Uh, yes."

"My dear…" Zelda chuckles. "…you sound old enough to know by now that in life, we get what we pay for."

I straighten my back. This is an adventure. It would be silly to give up on an adventure because of the cost of it. "Of course, yes. What's the address?"

She rattles it off. Of course, I didn't catch it, but thank god, Nina mouths that she knows where it is. I thank Zelda and the line goes dead.

"So, let me get this straight," Andrea says as we stumble along Chestnut Street in search of the nearest ATM. "We're going to withdraw four hundred freaking dollars from your account—"

"Oh, my God, say it a bit louder, don't you? The muggers in Philadelphia didn't hear you," Nina scolds.

"—and we're going to go to this stranger's home, and you're going to get a love potion. Is this really what's happening?"

"Look Killjoy, you can always go home, you know," Nina mutters.

For a moment, they glare at each other, then Andrea breaks into a big grin. "Hell, no. I wouldn't miss this for the world. This is like, the most interesting thing we've done in a long time."

"So? What are we waiting for?" Nina cries excitedly.

"Come you two crazies," Andrea shouts as she links arms with me and Nina. We continue to walk. Unsteadily.

Because we're all drunk. Andrea just takes longer to show.

While I withdraw the money, they both keep a watch, then wait for me to secure it in my purse. God, we are so obvious, it's a wonder the cops haven't stopped us to ask what we're up to. I'm pretty sure Nina thinks she's one of Charlie's Angels or something, looking back and forth at all times. As I put the money into my purse, Andrea spots a taxi and runs at it yelling.

It stops in front of us and we all pile into it.

Ten minutes or so later, the taxi pulls up and we find ourselves in a rather shabby neighborhood. Dark and a little eerie. If I wasn't so drunk, I think I might be scared right now.

"There can't be much demand for her potions," Andrea mutters, next to me.

"That must be it," I say as I make out the number 696 on one of the doors. The number 9 has almost fallen off, making it look more like 666. Creepy. Very creepy. I'm so glad the girls are with me. I pay for the cab and we all tumble into the street.

"This is nice," Nina says, looking up at the house and shifting her weight from one foot to the other.

"Yeah, I don't get a mass-murdery feel at all," Andrea adds sarcastically.

"Even if the potion doesn't work, we'll have a hell of a story to tell," I say.

It was good that we walked for a bit though. The cold air has cleared my head a little, so I don't feel as fuzzy as I did earlier. The money seems to weigh a ton in my purse. The psychic weight of it is much heavier than its physical mass.

I have to pretend to be a lot braver than I am when I

raise my fist to knock at the door. That slight motion pushes it open. She left it cracked for us.

"Here we go," Andrea whispers, patting my shoulder before giving me a gentle shove forward.

The door opens onto a long, dark hall lined with a couple of doors on either side. They're closed with only the lighting fixtures on the walls showing us the way, ornate iron sconces with little pink, beaded shades on each. The wallpaper is dark and our shoes click on the hardwood floor.

The door at the end of this hallway is open, revealing what I guess is the living room. The air here smells musty and it's cluttered with antiques and all sorts of bric-a-brac. There must be a fortune's worth in here, I think to myself. Or is it all old junk? It's hard to be sure.

The windows would look out onto the street we arrived at if they weren't covered with dark velvet curtains, the same sort of draperies which cover the walls. Lit candles sit on pretty much every flat surface. There's incense burning somewhere. It hangs heavy in the air and fills the room with a haze. I have to force myself to keep from fanning away with my hands.

"Come closer, my dear."

None of us noticed her until she spoke, meaning all three of us jump at the sound of her voice. No wonder it sounds so smoky. The woman is surrounded by actual smoke all the time.

She sits at an old, round wooden table partly covered by the same purple velvet that she's hung throughout the room. There's an honest-to-God black cat seated on the table which she slowly pets as her eyes take in the three of us—and we take her in, as well. Her long, glossy brown hair is streaked with gray, arranged in thick ringlets which cascade over her shoulders that are wrapped in a huge shawl. Gray eyes lined heavily in black under dark, perfectly arched brows. Her plump, ruby lips curve into a smile as she stands, revealing her purple robes. She is wearing a long skirt that hides her feet.

She fixes her eyes on me. "You are the one longing for love."

I wonder how she can be so sure. "Yes," I reply.

She beckons for me to follow her further into her lair.

When she raises one hand to shake, I wonder how she can even lift it considering the number of rings and bracelets she wears. They match her hoop earrings and multiple necklaces. In other words, she's magnificent and pretty much everything I would've expected.

"I am Madam Zelda," she announces with pride. "I welcome you to my home."

"I'm—Lauren," I whisper. "My friends, Andrea and Nina."

She acknowledges them, but barely. Lifting her chin, she announces, "They can sit. I have no need to speak with them. It is you who've come to me for the assistance from the other world which only I can provide."

Andrea chokes on a laugh behind me, and her soft groan tells me Nina elbowed her.

Zelda pretends not to notice or care, waving a hand toward a small sofa in the corner before turning full attention to me.

I feel like a prize cow getting looked over at the state fair. She takes in every last bit of me, walking around me in a circle. I expect her to ask to examine my teeth. I think she might even sniff my hair, but that could be my imagination trying to make sense of the absolute shit-storm of crazy I've walked into.

Once she's finished her examination, Zelda pulls out the chair sitting opposite hers. "Sit at the table, my dear.

Let us speak of he whose love you wish to obtain."

I do as I'm told because, hey, who wouldn't?

Zelda sits too, and that black cat jumps up in front of her as if on cue. It stares at me with its green cat eyes and I wonder for a second if it's actually thinking, actually forming opinions of me.

Maybe it's not incense Zelda's burning, because this makes no sense.

"First, the matter of payment." Zelda's eyes are sharper as she watches me fumble for my wallet—she counts the money quickly, red-nailed fingers flying over the bills.

Andrea snorts.

Nina shushes her.

"Very well, then." The money disappears into Zelda's ample bosom. "Tell me about this man."

I'm at a loss. "He's… my next-door-neighbor," I murmur, tucking my hair behind my ears. "He's handsome. Young. I've seen him walking in and out with rolls of blueprints under his arm. I think he's an architect."

"You think?" she asks, one brow arching even more than before. "You do not know?"

"I mean, I'm not stalking him or anything like that," I correct hastily.

"But you haven't spoken with this man? Haven't asked him about himself? You know nothing about him?"

Shit. My heart's sinking faster than a stone. "I— uh, no. I haven't really spent time with him. We've met once. This morning."

"You have a *crush* on him, then?" She almost spits it out like it's a dirty word.

"I-I—um maybe—no—I mean, well there is something there." And I think I just threw my money away.

Madam exhales loudly.

"What's so wrong with something? Every relationship has to start with *something*," Andrea says over my shoulder.

"There is a difference between love and a mere crush, child," Zelda points out, glancing at Andrea. "It is not advisable to play with love. Love is the greatest force imaginable. Love conquers all. Love is the strongest of all our emotions."

"All you need is love…" Andrea sings softly.

Nina giggles are muffled by her hand over her mouth.

"Enough! Silence!" Zelda raises her arms.

I would swear on the Bible that I feel a chill come over the room. The candle flames actually flicker in unison.

The girls go silent.

I think I might have just peed a little.

Zelda lowers her arms, staring at me as she does. "Your story is not unlike that which I've heard time and again. You are not unique, my dear, in your pining for a young man you know little about. There is no crime in this. The tea leaves will tell the true tale. The tea leaves never lie."

Chapter Five

LAUREN

"Tea leaves?"

At that precise moment, there's a whistling sound which makes us all jump.

Madam Zelda stands and takes a whistling kettle off an old stove in one corner of the room.

I turn to stare with wide eyes at the girls.

Nina makes a face.

"I knew you would come," she croaks.

I notice for the first time a teapot on the little table beside her, and two cups.

There is a tense silence while she makes the tea. Then she sits down opposite me again, pushes back her sleeves and pours a dark, strong looking brew into both cups.

I finally see the trace of a smile on her wrinkled face as she stares at me.

"Now, drink," she orders, "And tell me about this love of yours."

I lift the cup to my lips and hold my breath before downing the tea. Even though I'm not breathing, I can still taste how bitter it is.

Would it be rude to make a face? It would be rude to make a face.

Andrea and Nina stay silent, for once. I think the candle thing scared them.

I drink the bitter tea quickly and pass the empty cup back to her. Then I haltingly tell her as much about my neighbor as I can, given my limited knowledge of him. I'm doubting it's enough for her to make her decision, but it doesn't seem to bother her as she studies my teacup from different angles.

The cat jumps into my lap. Good thing I'm not allergic. I can only sit here, stroking its sleek fur, watching as Zelda weighs my future in her hands.

For a few moments more, she swirls the cup round and round, scattering the soggy remains around the inside of the cup. Zelda turns the cup this way, that way, examining the leaves in the bottom. "Interesting. Very interesting."

"Is that a good thing, or a bad thing?" I whisper.

"That depends," she murmurs. "I've seen these patterns before. Rarely, however. Once or twice."

"What—what do they mean?" I'm almost not sure I want to know, honestly. What if they say I'm going to lose my job, go into debt and become homeless?

She puts the cup down slowly. The air is full of the drama created by her. "Yes. You are ready for love. It is certain." She looks up at me, then rises from the table. Without a word, she sweeps out of the room, followed closely by her cat.

I turn and look at the girls.

They shrug.

The sounds of clattering, banging and the occasional cries of a cat come from the room next door.

"What the hell?" Nina whispers.

"I think we should haul ass out of here," Andrea hisses.

"Easy for you to say. You didn't spend four hundred dollars for this experience." Even though she has a point.

We all cringe as something heavy falls.

Moments later, Zelda returns, brushing dust from her robes. But she's holding a dark glass vial with cork stopper in one hand.

My eyes widen when I see it. "Is that…?" I ask.

"It is." She sits down again, placing the vial on the table.

I reach for it—then cry out in surprise when she slaps my hand back. "Hey!" I rub the spot where her hand made contact.

"It is not ready yet," she whispers. "Do not be greedy."

"Says the woman who charged four hundred dollars," Andrea mutters, and Nina mutters in agreement.

Zelda shoots them a cold glare before raising her hands over the vial. "I must imbue the potion with the magic needed to bring it to life." She closes her eyes, moving her hands in slow circles and humming. Loudly. Her body starts to undulate. The humming is even louder.

I don't know whether to laugh or leave.

When her hands slam against the table, the three of us jump. Nina even squeals.

Zelda's chest heaves up and down like she's just finished some huge physical feat. Her eyes pop open. "It is finished."

I blink, waiting for more. When nothing comes, I ask, "That's it? The magic is ready? Or something?"

"Indeed." She stares at me. "Well, take it."

Sorry, but I didn't want to get my hand slapped again. I reach for the vial, expecting it to tingle or sizzle in my hand after all that hocus pocus stuff. It doesn't. It's just a little glass bottle, like any other. I turn it upside down and can indeed see liquid moving around inside. "What should I do with it?"

"You must bake it into a treat. A cupcake or cookie would be best—the sweetness masks the slightly chalky taste of the potion, and the portion is perfect for a single person."

"She's obviously never seen me sit down with a cake," Nina whispers.

Zelda's eyes bore into mine. "You must use it in the next three days or it will become ineffective."

"Three days?" I ask, wondering how I'm supposed to get this to him in two days. Apology cupcake, maybe? 'Sorry You Stepped In My Dog's Poop' cookies?

"And what happens when he eats it?" Andrea asks.

Is it just me, or does she sound like she believes this for real? She's not joking anymore.

"The effect will be quite sudden, and quite serious." Zelda glares at me, her voice commanding. "Keep it safe. Use this power with care. Do not allow anyone else to eat the potion. If it ends up in the wrong hands or given to the wrong person, the consequences could be… *dire*."

I swear to God, the word echoes through the room like the reverberation of a gong. *Dire, dire, dire*. It sends chills up my spine, and not the good kind. It's enough to make me wonder if this was such a good idea. I'm messing with magic here.

This frightens me a little, and I open my mouth to question her about it, but she ignores me and continues, "Magic spells are not to be taken lightly. Now you may leave through the same door you came in from."

"Ok, bye then," I say, "Thank you—is there anything else I should know?"

"No. Go now." Zelda rises, motioning toward the door.

Yeah, she doesn't have to tell me twice. The three of us

haul ass down the hall and out the door. I don't think any of us breathes until we're in the elevator.

It could just be the smoke I've been breathing in since we walked into that living room, or the lingering effects of the vodka I drank earlier, but I could swear I hear laughter coming from the apartment when we close the door.

"Let's get out of here," Andrea says, clasping my hand. "This place gives me the creeps."

We step on to the road and as if by magic the thick, black clouds in the sky part and the moon shines through. All of us see it very clearly—it is not a round full ball of light, but a thin white crescent. Oh, crap! There is no full moon! And there was no reason for us to rush here tonight with my hard-earned money.

Nina gasps.

Andrea wisely keeps her mouth shut.

I've just been conned out of four hundred dollars. Yeah, this was one day I should not have gotten out of bed for.

Chapter Six

LAUREN

A dog's tongue laps on my face, dragging me from sleep.

"No...please, no. Have a heart, Draco." I turn my head to the side and that's not a good idea, since it feels like there's a marching band storming through my brain.

Draco doesn't care. He just jumps over my prone body, stretches out on the bed and starts licking from the other side. He's easy that way.

"I said, cut it out. I fed you when I got home." Crossing my arms over my face doesn't help. "And I took you out too, even though it was late at night and even though I hate walking around late at night. So don't tell me you need anything right this very minute."

But Draco just wants love. And licking. Lots of licking. The dog is a lick addict. He might need an intervention.

A brief opening of my eyes confirms my greatest fear...its morning, it's a bright morning, and my head feels like it's going to split straight open. Why did I drink that sixth or seventh martini? Even the fourth one is never a good idea, no matter how smart it seems at the time.

At least I had the foresight to leave a bottle of water on the bedside table, which I drink from very gladly. At least my stomach isn't churning.

The memories of the night flash before me. Yuck. I hold my head and groan, my mind still ticking away slowly. My heart suddenly sinks. Oh, my God. The gypsy woman. Zelda. Shit. I hope for a second it's some kind of night-mare. But nope, the memory solidifies. I gave her four hundred bucks.

"Draco, why am I so stupid?" I groan as my head sinks back into the pillow.

He snuggles in next to me, which is pretty much all he wanted to do in the first place, and stares at me with the same adoration he always stares at me with. It doesn't matter to him that I blew four hundred bucks last night.

"That's going to a lot fewer treats for you, little boy," I whisper, absently stroking his fluffy, white fur.

He sighs.

"I know. It was a very, very dumb thing to do. It seemed like a good idea at the time, though. You wouldn't understand it, but lots of things seem like a good idea when you're drunk." I open one eye and look down at him as his big, brown eyes are staring at me. "Like, you know when you're in the middle of eating your favorite treat and you're just completely blissed out and not thinking straight and everything in the world is awesome? Yeah. That sort of feeling."

But even Draco, a dog, wouldn't do something as stupid as I did. Four hundred dollars for a vial of what's probably nothing but tap water. Women like Zelda capi-talize on the loneliness of others to turn a quick buck. No wonder she was laughing when we left. Probably counting her money.

My purse is lying on the floor. I pick it up, scramble around in the bottom of it, and find the tiny glass vial. The liquid has a pink tinge to it and I ease out the cork, sniffing inside, but it doesn't really smell like anything. Maybe slightly sweet. I put it to one side and sigh. What a prize idiot! Spending insane amounts of money, I can't afford.

My head needs pain relief and my heart needs coffee. Or maybe it's the other way around. I drag myself out of bed and stumble towards the door.

Danny, my roommate's door is open. I guess he must have come back a day early. I look in, but it is empty. He is already up and out, probably at a yoga class or something similar. Since he went alcohol free, he's a changed man and its mornings like today when I wonder if I should take a leaf out of his book. Especially as I pick up the discarded items of clothing from the night before and toss them in the laundry basket. I have no idea how my shoes ended up where I found them; one in the kitchen and the other in the bathroom. But that could easily have been down to Draco rather than me.

I pour the coffee down my throat, fall back into bed, and drift off to sleep again. The phone wakes me up a couple of hours later, and I nearly fall out of bed trying to get to it. For some weird reason, I thought it might be work, but it is only Nina.

"How are you feeling today?" she asks with a dry chuckle.

"Probably about as good as you—but poorer. Considerably poorer."

"Come on. It's not that bad. You've spent more than that in a day at the mall. I was there. I remember."

"Yeah, but there's a difference between dropping that

sort of cash at the mall and blowing it away the way I did last night. I have nothing to show for it."

"You have the potion."

Which is sitting on the end table, staring at me. Blaming me. Laughing at me. "Yeah, well, whoopee doo."

"Come on…" She laughs. "I'm sorry. It was all my idea and I feel like garbage for even suggesting it, but she sounded so nice and helpful when I called her and I was very drunk last night too."

"You have a point there. It was all your idea and I think I will silently hold you responsible for the duration of our friendship."

She laughs. "Want to go halves?"

"Nah."

"You sure? Because I really don't mind."

That is what I love about Nina. She is a truly sweet natured person. "Nah. It was my decision. Thanks though."

"All right. So you spent some money. No big deal. You won't even feel it in a month or so. And you have a fantastic story…I mean, come on. I know I'll never forget what happened last night. And I plan to bring it up at your wedding someday. You know. When you marry the guy next door."

"Shut up," I groan, putting a hand over my eyes. "That's never going to happen. She's a con-woman pure and simple. She even lied about it being full moon last night."

"Yeah, but that's just a sales tactic. She was adding urgency and a sense of drama to the situation. The candles did all flicker at once when she yelled at us to shut up."

"You're right. That did happen. I think I peed a little when it did."

She giggled. "Oh, I'd be surprised if I didn't."

"Either she's really magic, or it was an effect she set up in the house. Who knows what she's set up behind those velvet curtains of hers?"

"Speaking of her house," Nina continues, "what was up with that? It was like a movie set."

"Yeah, that sounds about right," I say glumly.

"And the hoarder conditions in the kitchen. I assume from the noise in there, anyway."

We both laugh, and I feel a lot better. She's right…it's a crazy story, something the three of us will share for the rest of our lives, and how can you put a price tag on something like that?

"So. I have to ask. You know I have to ask."

I roll my eyes—which doesn't matter, because she can't see it. "Am I going to use it?"

"Yes."

"No," I say firmly.

"Lauren!"

"Nina!" I tease.

"Come on," she whines. "You went to all the trouble to get it and spent all that money."

"I thought this was going to be just a fantastic story we could all look back on and laugh over."

"What idiot told you that?"

"Lay off, okay? Please. It was a silly idea. I can't do something like that to a total stranger. Who knows what is even in that bottle. It could be poisonous."

"Why did you even buy it if you're going to punk out like this?"

"Because I was drunk and you guys pressured me."

"Andrea didn't want you to do it at all."

"Yeah, which is what pressured me," I mutter. "I wanted to prove her wrong."

"Gotcha. I still think it's worth a shot, though."

"Why?"

"Because how could she survive if she's a scam artist? Wouldn't word of mouth get around? I mean, this is the internet age, babe. If somebody's pizza shows up late, the first thing they do is go online to complain. I mean, they don't even eat the pizza right away, they're so busy going online to complain."

"You have a point."

"I say go for it. What do you have to lose?"

"Oh, I don't know. My self-respect?"

"Psh. Who needs that?"

"I do, if I'm going to keep living next door to Mr. Miller."

"So that's his name? I thought you two never really talked."

"That doesn't mean I can't check out his mail."

She laughs. "Stalker."

"Says the woman who wants me to trick him into taking a love potion."

I do feel better by the time we're off the phone.

My phone pings, and I'm lulled out of my TV trance.

Chapter Seven

LAUREN

I t's a message from Andrea:

Open the door. I've brought coffee and doughnuts!!

I open the door and she looks fresh as a daisy. Typical. She gives me a hug and hands me a steaming coffee. My third of the day. Hopefully this will be the one to make me feel human again.

Draco comes running into the hallway and jumps excitedly all over her.

"Hello, poo face." She fishes a treat from her purse and gives him a treat. He runs off it with it and she turns to me. "How's the head?"

"Pretty horrendous." I smile back, sheepishly. My eyes pan down her body as I admire her flashy workout leggings and then I groan as I realize why she's wearing them.

"You forgot about spin class, huh?" she smirks, reading the look of realization on my face.

"Completely," I have to admit. Ugh. I don't know if I

can face it. But I also don't know which is going to be harder – convincing Andrea that I'm not going – or actually doing the damn class.

"Chill, we have plenty of time, it doesn't start 'til four." She sits down and glances around. "Danny not back yet?"

"He is, but I think he must be at yoga or meditation or something like that."

"So he's still off the booze then? I'm impressed."

"Yeah, he's doing really well. It was getting kind of out of hand after his Dad died."

"It's great he's getting himself sorted. I do love party Danny, don't get me wrong. But he was a bit out of control."

"It's me that's getting out of control now. I know." I'm shaking my head. I'm suddenly struggling to hold back the tears. "I can't believe what I did last night, especially considering I might not even have a job soon. I really can't afford to throw that amount of money away on a drunken whim while I meant to be saving for our girl's trip," I say in a shaky voice.

"Aw, come here Laur."

She always calls me that when she's being extra nice. She puts her arms around me and pulls me towards her lean body. "It's not your fault some nasty con artist took advantage of you like that. It shouldn't be allowed. Some poor drunk girl looking for love. How dare she do that to you!"

I dismiss her unflattering description of me and get to the point. "Do you really think there's nothing in it?" I ask her gingerly.

"In the potion?" She takes my hand and looks at me earnestly. "No, I don't. I think it's a load of bullshit."

"Yeah. I guess," I sigh. I'm feeling more and more despondent about the whole thing.

"I blame Nina," she says, frowning, "Putting these ridiculous ideas into your head when you were smashed on cocktails."

"I don't blame anyone but me. I guess I really wanted to believe it. I knew I shouldn't but it just sounded so amazing. To make my neighbor fall in love with me! Can you imagine?"

"Look, if you really like this guy, why don't you just ask him out?"

Ha. It's so easy for Andrea. If she sees a guy she likes, she just goes up to him and starts talking to him. And then ignore his endless calls. I didn't understand her.

"I find it really hard to just approach men like that. I'm really assertive at work and when I get back service, but when it comes to men," I complain. "And anyway, I tried and look what happened. It couldn't have gone worse!"

"Don't let some silly incident with Draco put you off him." She sighs

At the mention of his name, Draco ambles into the room still licking his lips. Such a darling. I don't know what I would do without him and his cuddles. We make a fuss of him and I let him lick the foam from my coffee cup as I stroke his scraggy blond fur.

"Anyway…" Andrea continues. She's far too focused to let doggie cuddles distract her from our conversation. "When are you going to ask him out?"

"Ask him out?" I screech. "I thought I was just going to try and talk to him first?"

"And say what? You're not going to get to know him with the odd snippet of conversation in the driveway! And you have the perfect excuse now, anyway."

"I do?"

"Yes, you do! You say how sorry you are for the other morning and say that you hope he'll accept your dinner invitation as a way to make it up to him. He won't be able to refuse."

"Ugh. I just don't know if I'm up to it." I pause. "It's not my style."

"What is your style, Lauren? You want a boyfriend but you're too afraid to try and meet someone. You need to grow some balls, girl."

Her words hit a nerve and I'm a little shocked. She knows me so well. Too well, maybe. But she isn't finished yet apparently. She opens her mouth to continue. Oh god, what next?

"We're in the 21st century, babe. It's the most exciting time to be alive as a woman. We have more choices than ever. A woman ran to become the president, and you can't even ask a man over for dinner? You're letting our side down."

I have to laugh. "You think I'm a disappointment to the entire female population because I won't ask a guy to go out with me? I think that's a bit harsh. But…fine, whatever."

"You're coward, Lauren Appleton?" she accuses.

"No, I'm not.

"Yes, you are."

"I'm very brave for the things that matter."

"This matters a lot. What if he is your soul mate and you miss the opportunity because you are too chicken to ask him out."

"What about him asking me out?"

She starts squawking like a chicken.

I take a deep breath. "Fine, I'll do it."

"Do what?" she asks, her eyes lighting up.

"I'll ask him out," I confirm, already regretting it.

"Pinkie promise?" She grins, wiggling her little finger in my direction.

She's pushing it, now.

"Pinkie promise. As long as you drop it for the rest of the day. I'm actually looking forward to spin class now, so I won't have to listen to you anymore!"

She rolls her eyes and smiles deviously as I push the horrifying thought of asking my gorgeous neighbor out to dinner to the back of my mind.

"Oh no, it's raining," I suddenly say with dismay as I glance out of the window.

"No excuses," Andrea quickly tells me.

Jesus, she's a slave driver sometimes. At least we have her miniature car to whizz around town in, Draco on my lap. I couldn't deny him the hour spent being spoiled at the spinning studio reception area. They love him there and he adores the attention.

"You look perkier already," she says as I return to the room, Lycra-clad and ready to sweat out all of last night's sins and stupidity.

I feel a little better, I have to agree.

"Come on then Draco," I say as I scoop him up and follow Andrea out of the door.

She makes kissing noises as she points to my potential future date's door.

Shaking my head, I shove her towards the steps.

Chapter Eight

LAUREN

I t's amazing what a bit of exercise does to your mood, I think, as I bounce up the steps towards my home with Draco in close pursuit. I feel a million times better than I did this morning.

My phone pings, and I stop to check it. Danny:

Got your fave in for dinner, sweets. And latest Tits and Dragons downloaded too. See you later! Mwah

Fucking amazing. Best roomie ever. I swear he's telepathic sometimes. I was really hoping he'd be around tonight. I need to talk to him about my situation at work. I need a man's opinion.

Lunch is cheese and pepperoni pizza. One cheesy mouthful after the next until all the hard-won sense of wellness I got from the exercise earlier is gone and all I want to do is veg out in front of the TV. "Screw it," I say, and throw myself on the couch. The rest of the afternoon passes with me staring contentedly at the flickering screen.

It's late afternoon and I've binged for too long on

Netflix when Draco starts getting restless. There are no emails or messages for me from work and feeling pretty damn sorry for myself, I rouse myself from the warmth of the couch.

I need to take a Draco for a walk, but I really don't want to risk running into my neighbor just yet. I *will* ask him out, but not today. I hide behind the curtains and see his car isn't parked in its usual place. So unless yesterday's unlucky streak is still running, I won't meet him but even so, I get into my sneakers reluctantly. If there was any way for me to get outside without passing his door, I swear I would have.

But other than throwing Draco out of the window and jumping out myself after him, there's no other option that doesn't involve the dog doing his business on my floor. So we hurry our butts past his door on the way out and I'm extremely relieved when his car does not pull up.

I take Draco to the park and work up a good sweat. Hopefully, I burn off the pizza. Nearly an hour later, I head for home.

As I reach my home, I carefully scan the street ahead. Good, he is not home. Darting down the street I round the corner and run straight into a man, my foot landing on his. I jump off quickly and look up.

Oh, god. No. Fate can't be this cruel. It's *him*!

"You two have really got it in for these shoes, haven't you?" he notes, his beautiful green eyes twinkling deliciously. "I only just got them cleaned after the last incident."

"I'm so sorry about—that," I stammer while my face decides to flush like a traitor.

"I'm only joking," he says.

When he smiles at me like that I think I'm going to faint. Dimples appear in the cheeks of his beautiful chiseled face and his eyes crinkle up. He runs his hand through his deliciously glossy black hair and I think he might be the most masculine man I've ever set eyes on.

Broad shoulders, a jaw I could cut granite with if that's even a thing, broad shoulders, tanned skin in the middle of winter. But he's not one of those guys who goes tanning. I can tell, somehow. He probably just wills his skin to tan and his skin knows it has no choice but to obey.

He's just coming in from a workout, judging by the clothes he's wearing. Not the fancy stuff he was in when he stepped into Draco's poo. His green eyes travels down my sloppy, sweaty clothes and damn, why didn't I put on a little lip gloss, or something before leaving the house? Why am I such a shlub?

"Any gifts left for me on the welcome mat?" he asks, flashing a killer smile. I mean, absolutely killer and bathroom sink white. It reveals dimples in his stubbly cheeks too.

I want to run my fingers over that stubble. Maybe other parts of his body too. Oh, God! Why am I acting like such a desperado? "I'm very sorry about that. Really, really am."

"I should be the one apologizing to you for acting like such a jerk. I was having a bad day. It wasn't your fault that I lost my chill. I mean, I wouldn't have a dog of my own if stepping in shit was a nightmare."

"You have a dog?"

"Yeah! He's pretty quiet, though. He hardly ever barks."

"I was gonna say, I've never heard barking coming from over there."

"I don't hear barking coming from your place, either." He bends down to scratch poor, patient Draco behind the ears.

"He's pretty good too. Only barks when he feels threatened. I guess he likes you." Oh, sweet lord, am I flirting with him? Is that what this is? I'm not even good at it, why am I doing it?

"What's his name?"

"Draco."

"Ah, Harry Potter." He grins.

"Actually, that was my grandfather's name."

One gorgeous eyebrow rises. "Really?"

"No. I named him after a character from a book series."

He has a really nice laugh. It makes me feel warm all over.

"My dog's name is Tyrion."

"Game of Thrones!" I exclaim.

"Yep. He was the runt of the litter, so it sort of seemed to fit."

Jeez, I could get lost in those eyes of his. And he's a Game of Thrones fan. Could he possibly be more perfect? Is he even human?

"Well, it's nice to see someone so happy on such a rainy day. Keep smiling," he says as he turns to leave.

In my head, Nina urges me on, "I'm smiling now, but I had the morning from hell, I woke up completely hungover," I babble. What am I going on about? But he's waiting. Listening. "Yeah, but all good now, made it to spin class, and got a night in with the best roomie ever tonight. And Draco of course." I grin.

"Draco. Nice to officially meet you." He bends down.

I'm so proud of Draco as he lifts a paw to greet him. What a champ.

"Did you say roomie?" he asks casually, "The guy you live with? I assumed you were together."

"Oh, no!" I reply. Maybe too quickly. "We're just

friends. Good friends! But nothing else. Ever." *Shut up*. "He bats for the other side. Absolutely has no interest in me." *SHUT UP.*

He smiles slowly.

Oh, wow. That smile.

"I was going to ask you something, actually," I continue, looking away from those very distracting dimples. *I can do this!* "I really wanted to make it up to you for, you know—your shoes, and the inconvenience and everything. Would you like to come to dinner one night? Maybe even… tomorrow night?" I dare to look up at him and let my eyes meet his again.

He looks really amused.

I don't know if that's a good sign.

"I mean," I rush on, "it's my way of apologizing for the dog poo incident. And maybe we can introduce the dogs, while we're at it." I'm really stretching this, pulling out all the stops. Using my dog as a bribe. It's not up there with buying a potion, but close.

"I wouldn't dream of saying no," he drawls. "And talking of introductions. I'm Jackson. Jackson Miller." He extends a hand.

His clasp is firm and warm. I die a little inside. My voice comes out squeaky. "Lauren. Lauren Appleton."

He said YES! What? Nina is clapping her hands and doing cartwheels in my head.

He smiles and I nearly melt into the ground. "Tomorrow night sounds good. I'll bring a bottle."

"Great!" I reply grinning like a Cheshire cat. "Okay. Any, um, dietary things I should know about? Restrictions, allergies?"

"I'll eat anything except fish."

"Gotcha." I practically skip to my door. I turn around quickly and yell, "Six-ish?"

"See you then!" he calls back.

Approximately fifty cannons go off in my head all at once. I can barely hear myself think.

He flashes one more super sexy smile before he continues on his way.

I close the door behind me and sink to the floor. What just happened? My heart is thumping in my chest and my cheeks are straining from the involuntary grin plastered across my face. "I did it, Draco!" I yell. "I'm a 21st century woman!"

I grab my phone and text Andrea and Nina:

Asked hot neighbor on date! He said YES!! No potion involved. Go me!

Chapter Nine

JACKSON

Well, well, well, the bearded guy living with her is *not* her boyfriend.

I smile to myself as I put my key into my door. Yeah, she's a little flaky. But cute. Definitely very cute. I'm not in the market for a girlfriend, but it's never a bad idea to make friends with the next-door neighbor.

It was gutsy of her to hit me up. She looked like she was about ready to fall over and die from embarrassment just from asking me. I've been meaning to apologize for being such a rude fucker myself. Not that I flip out anywhere except in my head, but still. Shit happens. Literally.

I push open the door and Tyrion is already spinning in circles with sheer unadulterated joy. As always. There's something to be said for somebody being that excited to see you when you get home. I went a really long time without this in my life.

"Hey, boy!" I say with a chuckle, crouching in front of him so he can sniff me. He starts smelling in earnest. "You smell Draco? You're gonna hang out with him tomorrow night while I hang out with his mom.

Shit! Where did that come from?

I'm not looking for a relationship. I've got no place for a girlfriend in my life right now. My existence is a mess presently. I'm up to my eyeballs with work and I'm living in this temporary accommodation without all my stuff because my apartment is being redone. No, I do not need the added complication of a relationship.

Not even without one as cute as Miss Appleton.

Even so.

No, Jackson, no.

I remember the landlord mentioning her when I came in to look at the house. Nice girl, he said, quiet and keeps to herself. No parties. All of that sounded good at the time and still does, since I need peace and quiet.

Not that a drink with the guys is off-limits, and in fact… oh, damn. I was supposed to meet up with Josh and Pete tomorrow night. I completely forgot. I occurs to me that I could cancel with Lauren, but I don't want to come off as a complete jerk. Well, that's my excuse and I'm sticking to it.

I put food into Ty's bowl and get into the shower. As soon as I'm out, I dial up Joe. I hear crying the second he picks up, before he even says hello. "Sorry," he calls out over the cacophony. "Teething. You know how it is."

No, I don't. I've heard how it is, since my friends are now of the age, where having kids has become a reasonable next step, but I've never been through it.

"I won't keep you long," I promise, mostly because I don't really feel like hearing the baby squall for much longer. "I'm not going to be able to make it out tomorrow night. I'm sorry, man."

"Wait. Wait, wait, wait. I'll just go lock myself in the bathroom." The sound of the baby's cries gets quieter until it goes away entirely.

Poor guy. I glance over at Tyrion, who's lying on the floor and licking himself. A dog is more than enough for me.

"Shit, this is the only place in the house I can get a minute of peace, Jackson. You honestly are backing out on getting drinks tomorrow night? Because I get out like, once in a blue moon anymore and I've been looking forward to it ever since we decided to hang out."

"You'll still have Pete with you."

"Oh, well. No big deal, I guess." He sighs.

"I'll make it up to you, man," I say feeling like a douche for cancelling on him. I'll meet you for happy hour some night this week. Or whenever is good for you."

He chuckles. "Wow, since when do you leave the office early enough to go to a happy hour?"

"I can make an exception. Gimme a call and let me know what's good for you, okay?"

"Right man, got to go."

I hear the yelling get louder so I quickly say my byes and end the call. I have a ton of work waiting for me on my table. I need to focus.

I also need to stop thinking about the girl next door and the way she smiles. The way she blushes whenever our eyes meet. She's definitely cute. Maybe even hot, though I've only ever seen her wearing bulky coats and scarfs, since we've only ever run into each other while she's on her way out with the dog.

Tyrion eventually scratches at my ankle, signaling that he needs to go out for a walk. I find myself looking at her door while I'm locking mine, wondering what she's doing in there. What's her life all about? What does she do with herself on a Saturday evening? What does she do for fun?

Fuck, I have stop this shit. She's just the girl next door. I'll have dinner with her tomorrow and that will be the end of that. Before the month is up, I'll be out of here, anyway.

Chapter Ten

LAUREN

As I get out of the shower, I hear the door swing open and then crash shut again. That can only mean one thing…Danny's home!

"Hey sweets," he yells. "You here?"

"Hey you!" I cheer, running towards him and giving him a big hug.

He's wearing a particularly brash cap today, but he throws it to one side now that he's home. He's not conscious of his increasingly receding hairline around me. He's certainly not lacking in the facial hair department though and I give his beard an affectionate tug.

I start to pick up the bags of shopping he's surrounded by, peeking at the goodies he's bought. He's certainly not one to scrimp on groceries, we could feed a small army!

"You're not drinking again, are you?" I ask, as he lifts a bag clinking with bottles.

"Noooo, this isn't alcohol, it's kombucha. Amazing stuff."

"I see." I'm glad he hadn't succumbed. And besides, I definitely didn't feel like drinking tonight.

"So, what's new?" he asks. "I feel like I haven't seen you for years."

"I know, I've missed you! How was vacation?"

"Really good. Incredibly relaxing. I spent it mostly in group meditation."

I scrunch up my nose. "That's what you call a vacation?"

"Don't knock it until you try it. How was the head this morning, by the way?" he asks, winking.

My eyes widen. "How did you know?"

He blows me a kiss. "Well, let me see. Clothes everywhere, the half-drunk pint glass of Berocca next to the sink… all very important clues."

I'm scrunching my face up. "Yeah, I guess it was pretty obvious now that I think about it."

"So, the usual terrible trio? I miss those girls. Well, Nina anyway."

"Yep, who else? And they miss you too! You know, you can still come and hang out with us in a bar and not drink."

"I'm not sure I'm quite at that stage yet… but how about we all go to yoga tomorrow morning instead? I've been invited to a sunrise class on a friend's rooftop terrace."

"It sounds amazing, if a little early…." I hesitate. I really should do more yoga, but… sunrise? On a Sunday? I think not.

"Oh, come on! It's good for the body, the mind, *and* the spirit to get up with the sun."

"I'm sure Andrea will go with you," I offer. I'm not budging on this one.

"Hmmm, Andrea. I like her. You know I do. But I think you and Nina balance her out a bit. Alone, she can be a little…well, brash."

I giggle. Andrea and Danny don't see eye to eye about a lot of things, and he doesn't really appreciate her business-like way of solving problems.

"She's just not very spiritual," he goes on. "I mean, she told me that the only reason she practices yoga is for the stretching. She doesn't get it at all!"

I just smile. I don't want to get into a discussion about Andrea right now. Especially when there are more pressing issues to discuss. "Listen, I need to ask you opinion on something?"

"Shoot," he says.

So I tell him how my shoe landed on the Mr. Montfort's face. His eyebrows fly up into his receding hairline, but he doesn't say anything until I end with the all-important question, "So what do you think? What would you do in my shoes?"

He shrugs. "Quite frankly. I wouldn't do anything."

I look at him curiously. "Really?"

"Yeah. I don't think you should grovel to your boss or team mates either. You should go in on Monday with your head held high."

"Did you actually get the gist of my story? I've lost the project that everybody was counting on. My boss was sobbing into his palms when I left his office."

"Your boss is too heavily invested in the outcome. He can't see the forest for the trees."

"What do you mean?"

He sits on a stool and leans his elbows on the island top. "You said your company's software is miles better than your competitors, right?"

"Absolutely," I agree immediately.

"Then you have nothing to worry about. The way I see it, if Mr. Monfort were going to be petty and not give your company the job because of an unfortunate accident, he wouldn't have let you carry on. He didn't get to where is he is today by not putting his company before anything else."

I nod and smile slowly. Of course, Danny is right. I knew he would make me feel better. "So you think I should brave it out on Monday."

"Hell, yeah. That's what I'd do."

I grin. "Okay, that's what I will do. Thanks, Danny."

He grins back. "That's my girl. Now, I've got to jump in the shower."

"Umm…Danny?"

"Yeah?"

"I was going to ask you something else too…" I start, tentatively.

He now looks really curious. "This sounds interesting. What is it?"

"Well, I kind of have a busy day tomorrow… and I was wondering if you're going to be around tomorrow evening?"

He thinks for a second before he replies, "There's a dinner slash poetry reading thing at this place in Haight-Ashbury, but I can change my plans if you wanna hang out? Or do you want to join?"

"No, no… actually I was hoping you might be out… I have someone coming over for dinner."

His eyes shine with interest. "Someone?" he asks, raising his eyebrow, "Like a date, you mean?"

"Yes, a date." My stomach flutters at the thought of it.

"Who is he?" he demands.

"You'll never guess who."

"Did you meet someone last night?"

I shake my head.

"Not Mr. Sexy and Mysterious from across the hall?!" he exclaims.

"No way. How did you know!?" Maybe all this spiritual stuff Danny was into really did make him a bit telepathic.

"Don't think I haven't noticed the way you lust over him!"

"I have not been lusting over him."

"Yes, I believe you have."

"Stop it."

He grins from ear to ear. "I'm impressed, honey!"

I reach out my hands and reciprocate his double high five. I can't control the size of my grin either as I'm not only feeling pretty pleased with myself, I also feel quite empowered too.

"I love this new confident you!" he gushes.

"Actually, it's Andrea who should take the credit. She basically made me pinkie promise that I would ask him out."

He rolls his eyes, "And how did she do that?"

I hesitate and sigh. I knew I'd have to tell him at some point, so it may as well be now. "I did something very stupid last night…"

"Oh?"

I pull a fake grimace and then smile. I'm actually feeling remarkably blasé about the whole gypsy malarkey now. First of all, I might not be losing my job after all so it's only money I've lost. Also, if not for the gypsy and the ensuing mess, I definitely would not have gotten the guts to ask Jackson out.

I sure as hell know Danny is going to love the story so I start from the beginning. From where I know he will appreciate. From Nina's penis problems. Danny is in rapture. He's always a perfect audience, it's one of the many reasons I love him so much. I'm at the point where I'm handing over the cash, but still only encouraging 'ooh's' and 'ah's' have come out of his mouth.

"So, what happened then?" he asks me, like I've missed the end of the story or something.

"I just got conned out of four hundred bucks!"

He shrugs. "Didn't she give you the potion?"

"Yeah, she did. I have it," I say, a little surprised he's not baulking at the amount of cash involved.

"So, what's the problem?"

"Danny, she's a con artist. I was slurring all over the place and she must have realized I was already more than half drunk so she lured me to her house and sold me a vial of bullshit."

"Said Andrea," he replies, looking at me knowingly.

I laugh. "You know us all too well sometimes." I give him a nudge. "So, do you really think it could work then? I mean, it just looks like pinkish water."

He puts on a deep voice and says, "Seeing is not always believing, my dear. And believing is not always understanding."

"Huh?"

He sighs. "You have to trust that some people in this world are blessed with a heightened spiritual sense than the rest of us. They are ultra-connected somehow and they can guide spirits together, and do all sorts of things that we just have to accept we will never understand."

I study his face looking to see if he is messing with me, but those dark brown eyes of his seem completely genuine.

"Look, sweets. Whether you believe in the powers of the potion or not, what have you got to lose? You may as well try it."

"What? No, I can't," I say, my heart suddenly beating a little faster.

He nods and goes wide-eyed. "So, let's see. The gypsy woman told you to give it to the 'intended' aka Mr. Sexy and Mysterious from across the hall, before the full moon, right?" He grabs his schedule, and flicks through it, then gasps dramatically. "That's tomorrow!"

I stare at him in amusement.

"It's meant to be," he whispers.

"Do you really think I should give it to him?" I ask curiously.

"Why not? Do you like this guy, or not?"

"Of course, I do. I mean, he's gorgeous." My stomach flutters at the thought of him. I still can't believe he's coming over for dinner tomorrow.

"Then there's nothing more to be said about it. Apart from how you're going to get it in him? So that he wants to get *in* you!" He makes a crude gesture with his pointed index finger.

I whack him hard. "Quite frankly, Mr. Daniel Purdy, I'm shocked at you. I can't believe you would encourage me to do something that would obstruct someone else's freedom of choice."

"Excuse me. You just said it was a load of old baloney. I'm just trying to jazz up your life."

"Regardless, I will not be using the potion."

"Fine. Do you mind if I keep the potion and use it on someone I fancy?"

I giggle. "You don't need a love potion. You already have too many men falling at your feet and begging to be your humble servant."

"This is true, but I need a more permanent addition to my harem."

"Take it." I walk to the living room, grab the vial and give it to him.

"Thanks," he says, "Okay, then. I'll go have my shower and we'll get started on cooking dinner." He starts walking away then, turns back. "What will you make for dessert tomorrow?"

I shrug. "Don't know yet."

"How about those delicious red velvet cupcakes with your mother's famous frosting? Everybody loves them."

I make a face. "Except me."

"How about you bake some for him and me, and I'll help you make a batch of vanilla ones for you." He smiles winningly.

I smile back. It's hard to say no to Danny. "Okay."

"Great. You'll see, with one bite of those and he'll never be able to resist your charms."

"If I didn't love you so much I would be insulted by that comment."

"But you do love me so much, so chill. You think we have everything we need?"

"Aw, you're such a star!" I give him a big bear hug and then go to look through our fridge and cupboards. "Yeah, I reckon we have everything."

"Okay, I'm off. Start chopping these," he says as he throws me an onion then a couple of tomatoes and grins. "We've got a busy night, sweets. Remember, we've got two episodes of Tits and Dragons to catch up on."

"It's called Game of Thrones," I reply, sinking a sharp knife deep into the onion.

Yep, Danny really is the best roomie ever.

Chapter Eleven

LAUREN

I open my eyes feeling so much better than the day before. A shiver of excitement runs through me when I think about the day ahead. Then I sit up in bed in alarm. "Draco?" I call.

He replies with an affectionate yap from the floor. He potters around to my side, tongue hanging out. Such a cutie.

"Come here, you gorgeous doggie," I say, patting the space beside me.

He makes to jump up, but stops in his tracks.

"Aw, Draco."

I've been worried about this day when he would eventually be unable to make it up onto my bed. The thought of no longer having my doggy lick-wake me every morning makes me feel sad. I lean down and scooping him up, lye back down with him on top of me.

"You love a tummy rub, don't you!" I say as I spoil him with attention. He makes those little sounds of lazy pleasure until I stop and tell him, "Okay, that's it now. We have to go shopping."

I wander into the kitchen and find a note from Danny on the fridge door:

Hey sleeping beauty.

Was going to wake you but you looked too peaceful! Feather picked me up and we took all the cupcakes and left just one for Jackson. We'll have them after yoga. Hope that's cool! Meeting Andrea there so will give her some too. Going straight to Josh, so won't see you till tomorrow. Love ya lots, good luck for tonight!!!!

Btw: Brian will be coming around later to repair your car. Leave the car keys under usual brick.

I look in the cake tin and check that the pink-cased cupcake is still there. Yes. Good. My stomach flutters a little thinking about tonight. But no time for that now.

After a quick shower and a coffee for me, and some 'extra healthy', high-protein, ridiculously expensive doggy biscuits for Draco, we're off and walking briskly down the street. The sunshine is blazing, but the air is chilly. I shiver as I think about Danny's sunrise yoga session. Well, Andrea's too. I knew she'd jump at the chance to go after I messaged her about it last night.

I pull Draco away from some garbage he's taking an unhealthy interest in, and we turn down Grant Avenue. I always gravitate towards China town for grocery shopping, rather than going to one of the big stores. I guess I just love the hustle and bustle, although it's definitely easier with Draco too. I tie him up at the entrance of one of my usual stores and grab a basket.

By the time we get home, my phone is lit up with new messages, all from the usual suspects: Danny, Andrea,

Nina, my Mom! It's nice to feel loved. I scroll through quickly.

Danny: *Wake up! Come to yoga!!*

Clearly, that didn't happen.

Danny: *Cupcakes are delicious!!*

Andrea: *Hey lazybones, why no yoga?*

Nina: *OMG are you excited about tonight??? Are you gonna use the potion?? Are you around for brunch? We have to talk! I'll come to your place at noonish??? xxxxxxx*

I check the time. It's just past eleven. I send her a quick message to confirm. I could do with some of Nina's excited energy before tonight.

Mum: *How are you my darling? I haven't seen you for ages! Are you busy tonight?*

Ugh, Mum. Not tonight. I'll text her later.

"Well, then Draco. Are you gonna help me prepare for tonight?"

He looks up at me thoughtfully and then settles down into his bed next to the sofa.

I smile at him. "Nope, I thought not. Guess it's just me then."

I start unpacking groceries. I have to make sure dinner is impeccable.

Chapter Twelve

LAUREN

"It smells amazing in here!" Nina cries out as she steps through the door.

"Thanks." I grin, returning her hug. "I've managed to pretty much get it all done I think!"

"What are you making? It smells like chicken." She's sniffing the air as she throws her coat to one side and flicks her beautiful dark ringlets around.

Sometimes, I think she's such a flirt that she flirts with me without even realizing she's doing it. "Yep, chicken cacciatore with roasted rosemary potatoes."

"Well, if that's not the way to a man's heart, then I don't know what is!"

"This, maybe??" I say to her, opening a cake tin to reveal the last beautiful red velvet cupcake Mom's special cream cheese frosting piped into careful swirls on top. It looks quite luscious if I say so myself. "This cupcake recipe has won awards."

"Hmm…imagine how much better it would be with a bit of love potion in it."

I shake my head decisively. "Nope."

"Come on. Why won't you give the Gypsy's potion a chance?"

"Because I have principles, Nina. There is no way on earth I am tricking him in falling in love with me. I wouldn't even have gone to the gypsy if I hadn't been so drunk." I take a deep breath. "Yup. Principles. That's me."

She sighs. "All right. It looks real pretty. Are you excited?"

"Excited but nervous… I'm worried we won't have anything to talk about. What if we have nothing in common?"

"Just ask him questions about himself. Men always love talking about themselves." She gives me a knowing look and smiles. "I hope he's not into old tanks and guns though! I told big cock it's not going to work, by the way."

"Oh, I'm sorry. How do you feel?"

"I'm fine. I'm relieved actually. And I have a blind date tomorrow with a friend of a friend from work anyway! So onwards and upwards."

This girl never ceases to amaze me. "It doesn't take you long, does it!?"

"The best way to get over someone is to get under someone else!" she replies with a grin.

"Cheers to that," I agree, and we clink our coffee mugs together.

"Did you wanna go out for brunch?" I ask her. "The other option is leftover Thai green curry from last night, and… you can help me figure out what to wear tonight!"

"Mmm…Thai green curry, yes please! And I know you're gonna need my help dressing." She eyes me up and down. "Please don't tell me this is the kind of stuff you were wearing when you asked him out.

I look down at my patterned leggings, neon pink

Nike's, and oversized hoody. "Um, similar, I guess," I tell her.

She tuts and shakes her head. "Take me to your wardrobe." She holds out her hand for me to take, with a hint of seduction.

This girl just oozes sex appeal. I'll take whatever help I can get. I take her hand, pull her up, and we head to my bedroom.

She pulls open the door of my wardrobe with a look as though a huge spider is going to crawl out of it. It's not like she hasn't seen the inside of my wardrobe a million times before! She fingers each item, making little disapproving noises and shaking her head. Finally, her fingertips make contact with something they approve of.

I groan as she shakes out a Jessica Rabbit style cocktail dress, an item I sadly bought and never wore. I feel like she probably knows how many times I've tried it on in my room alone, twirling in front of the mirror and wishing I had somewhere to wear it.

"Don't be ridiculous, I'm not wearing that!"

"Oh, it would be marvelous! He would be knocked out! Can you imagine the look on his face when he opens the door and sees you standing there in that!?"

"He'll think I'm ridiculous!"

There is no way I'm wearing that dress.

She stares at me with raised eyebrows.

"Nope. There is no way I'm wearing that," I tell her, shaking my head. "It's a casual cozy meal at home. We're not going to a ball!"

Nina sighs heavily and shoves it back in.

Chapter Thirteen

LAUREN

I scan my eyes over the living room, checking if I've missed anything. I've set the table for two, with wine glasses, napkins. I've lowered the blinds a little and there are a few candles flickering on the windowsill. I hope I've got the vibe right. Cozy and a little bit intimate. The rich, meaty aroma of sparerib ragu simmering quietly fills the air.

The sound of a knock on the door makes my stomach flutter. Oh, my goodness. He's early, I think. But checking my phone, he's actually exactly on time. Well, that's a good sign, I guess. I check myself quickly in the mirror. I decided on a simple black top and slim fitting jeans. I take a deep breath, and open the door.

As our eyes meet, he's already smiling and I can't help but smile back.

"Hey, you made it," I say. "Come in!" My heart is thumping and I can't believe how hard. "I hope you didn't think it was weird that I invited you around so early for dinner! I always have dinner early on Sunday, I guess. We don't have to eat yet, if you're not hungry."

Am I babbling? I can't tell. The nerves are getting to me.

"It's cool, so do I." He grins, his eyes twinkling even more than in the hallway just the day before. "And actually, I'm starving!" He comically rubs his stomach, but as he does his T-shirt rises revealing just a little of strip of his tanned, flat stomach, a section of the trail of little dark hairs leading down from his navel and disappearing at the start of his jeans.

Oh, my goodness. I need to pull myself together.

"Great," I say, hoping he doesn't notice my shaky voice. "What would you like to drink?"

"Water for me to start with, but I brought you this." He thrusts a bag towards me.

Peeking inside, I find two expensive-looking bottles of red and white wine.

"I didn't know what we'd be having for dinner."

"It's okay. I don't ascribe to the whole red-with-red-meat rule, anyway. I'll drink whatever tastes good." I fill up a glass with water. "Here," I say, holding the glass out to him.

He takes it and drinks deeply.

God, I'm admiring his physique again as he finishes the glass. I've only ever seen him in work or gym clothes before, but today he's wearing jeans and a black polo shirt. His bicep flexes as he drinks and I feel my knees wobble slightly beneath me. Thank goodness, I decided to stick to jeans. I manage to stifle a snort with laughter as I imagine myself sitting in front of him in my Jessica Rabbit dress.

He looks at me. Quite strangely, I have to add.

Jeez, be normal. I take his glass and refill it for him. "Did you just work out?" I ask stupidly.

"Yes, do you mind if I bring another guest. A four-legged one?" he asks. Draco is already sniffing at his pant legs, jumping around. "Does your boy like meeting new friends? I know Tyrion always does."

"Sure thing." I put the white wine in the fridge and open the bottle of red at the dining room table while he fetches his dog and brings him back. The two of them sniff each other for a long time, with Jackson and me watching closely, then run off to play.

"Whew." I laugh as I hold up the bottle in a silent question.

He nods, so I pour him a generous swig and hope I don't sweat through my top. It only took me seven tries to find something I thought was acceptable for tonight.

"Well, now you're stuck with me." He grins as I hand over the glass.

"What do you mean?" Damn it, I'm blushing. I haven't even had any wine yet, so I have nothing to blame it on.

"Once Tyrion makes a friend, they're stuck with him. Which ropes you in by association."

Thank you, Tyrion. "I guess I'll have to deal with it, won't I?" I motion to the sofa.

He takes a seat and looks around.

Meanwhile, I'm observing him. The man can wear a pair of jeans and a T-shirt, I'll give him that. His arms, shoulders and chest are clearly defined even in a sweater, and his big powerful hands…

"Your roommate not in tonight then?" he observes, watching me watching him.

"No, Danny's out with a friend," I say, covering my embarrassment by waving my hand vaguely towards the door. Hmm… I wonder why he asked that? I feel a little bit crazy. Like a black widow spider, I've lured this innocent man into my empty house and now I'm trying to seduce him. Andrea's voice is in my head, telling me it is the 21st

century and women have started taking the initiative and going for what they want.

The dogs chase each other back and forth and the bread warms in the oven as I take a seat opposite him. I tell him that it won't be long and his stomach suddenly growls loudly.

He clutches it and apologizes.

I giggle and he laughs too.

"I didn't realize you were *that* hungry! I'm so sorry, I'll go dish up now."

We take our places at the table. He smiles and looks into my eyes as our legs touch ever so slightly under the table. His eyes are a mesmerizing green.

"Hope you like sparerib ragu with fettuccine. It's very high carbs, I'm afraid."

"Don't let the way I look fool you." He grins, lifting a massive forkful of fettuccine from the bowl. "I believe in balance. I love tucking into a bowl of pasta." His eyes then widen at the first bite of pasta, studded with chunks of carefully shredded short rib. "Wow. Heaven."

My cheeks flush, along with the rest of me. "Really?"

"Yeah, really. I think I might have to make a habit of having dinner here."

I beam with happiness. "My mom taught me to cook. She'd treat it like a cooking show as if she was on TV. It was fun. Then it was Lauren's turn."

"Lauren," he whispers with a half-smile. "An old-fashioned name. I like it."

"After my grandmother," I explain. "I think she's the one who taught Mom to cook too."

"You have a tight family?"

"Oh, sure." I probably bore him half to death with stories about family holidays and dinners and other memories—but then he counters with memories of his own, and before I know it the candles on the table are all but burned out, and we're seated in front of empty plates but still talking. I could talk to him all night.

I could do a lot of things with him all night, if he was so inclined. I only thought I wanted him before this. Now I know I do, because I'm getting to know the real person behind that body and that face. He's a pretty amazing person, and I know now, that he is only temporarily going to be my neighbor. He lives uptown in an amazing penthouse that he's redesigning. He showed me the pics. I remember now Danny remarking that he didn't belong in this neighborhood.

"Want me to help with the dishes?" he offers.

"Let's forget the dishes for now," I suggest, standing. "How about something sweet?"

He smiles with a wink. "I could definitely go for something sweet right about now. I have a huge sweet tooth."

Oh, sweet Jesus, he's the sexiest freaking thing alive. I'm a bit of prude, Andrea will tell you, but at this moment, I'm seriously tempted to clear the table with a sweep of my arms and throw myself at him. Literally, the only thing stopping me is the knowledge that the dogs would hurt themselves on the broken dishes. Or the fact, that I am the biggest coward in the world.

"Go make yourself comfortable," I murmur, pointing to the couch.

The pups have tired themselves out, both of them snoozing on an armchair. Jackson pats both of their heads as I go to the kitchen.

I smile to myself as I plate them, thinking of that crazy idea I had of putting a love potion in his cupcake. To think Nina actually thought it was a good idea. He's not just gorgeous and sexy. He's smart, funny, real and he loves his dog... oh, jeez, how can I not fall for somebody who loves his dog that much? He isn't just the sexy hunk next door anymore. He's a person, a real person, and he deserves better than to be tricked.

Anyway, it was just funny-smelling water in that vial. Nothing else. Very, very expensive water. Oh well, I guess the gypsy needed the money more than me. I have a great life. I don't need a love potion. I'm doing just fine without it. I bring back the cupcakes – after making sure to smooth down my hair and adjust my bra beforehand – pushing my boobs up and out a little. It can't hurt.

I lower our cupcakes to the coffee table.

"Ooh, what's this?" he asks, holding up the plate in front of him to admire.

"Red velvet. My mom's specialty. You have to try it. It's won awards at baking contests."

"Really?" He begins to unwrap it. Suddenly, he lets out a yawn. A big one. "I'm sorry," he says, smiling apologetically.

"I know, I'm pretty boring…" I pretend to chuckle, but I'm crushed and wondering if it's me. Am I boring the hell out of him?

"You're not." He licks frosting from his fingers. "I'm just exhausted. It's been a long week, and I guess it's catching up to me."

"Tell me about it. I had a hell of a week, myself."

He glances toward the kitchen. "Could I maybe have some coffee? I know it's asking a lot after you made that incredible dinner…"

"Oh, of course!" I'm off the couch before he even has the chance to finish the request. I want to spend as much time as I can with him, since I doubt I'll get the chance again. He's leaving in two weeks and men like him don't usually end up with women like me.

In the kitchen, I look at my phone. Two new messages.

Andrea: *Good luck! But DON'T give him that stupid potion. You've got this! Just be your gorgeous self!*

Nina: *OMG I'm so excited! How's it going?? Did you give him the love cake yet??? Love you xxxxxxx*

I send Mom a quick message:

Hey Mom! Sorry about late reply. Busy! Can we do tomorrow instead? Love you x

She doesn't need to know about my date. She'd only get way too excited and ask loads of questions.

As I am pouring the coffee into two cups, my cellphone rings. I glance at it not intending to pick it up, but when I see that it is Danny, I immediately take the call. He would never call if it weren't urgent. I snatch up the phone. "What's up, Danny?"

"Please don't be angry with me, but I put the potion into the red velvet cupcake."

My stomach lurches. "What?"

"I don't know what I was thinking, but I just wanted you to be happy, you know?"

"I can't believe you did that?" I whisper fiercely.

"Sorry. I know you really like this guy and I just wanted to increase your odds."

"I'll talk to you tomorrow," I say tightly and end the call. I start walking towards the living room. Even if it's never going to work, it's still the wrong thing to do. Who knows what is actually in that vial? Zelda could've given me anything.

Oh God, I have to get there before he eats the cake. And now my palms are sweaty and my stomach's in even tighter knots than before.

I almost forget to bring the coffee back into the living room, I'm in such a hurry to stop him from eating that stupid cupcake. I'll come up with a reason why he can't eat it. Like… I just remembered that I forgot to add sugar to the batter or something that'll make me look flaky, but will at least keep him from choking and foaming at the mouth on my living room sofa.

"Hey, you know what…?" I trail off as I enter the room, and I just might lose my dinner all over the floor.

Because there, on the coffee table in front of Jackson, is a plate with nothing but a paper wrapper in the middle and a few crumbs left from what used to be a cupcake.

Chapter Fourteen

LAUREN

O h, shit. Shit and hell. I can't believe this.

What's he going to do? Start twitching? Convulsing? Choking? Jesus Christ, they'll be able to trace his death to me. The cupcake. And the girls, they were there when I bought the potion. The cops might pressure them to testify against me. They'll find me guilty. I'll end up in the electric chair. Oh, wait they don't do that inhumane thing anymore. Oh, my God, I'll get injected with poisonous chemicals. A fitting end for a poisoner.

What am I supposed to do now? I'd have to drop Danny in it and I don't want to do that.

I could pretend we didn't know what would happen to him. Yes, I think it would be better if people thought I was an idiot for believing in love potions than to think I'd poison somebody. I'd rather have them laugh at me than put me in the electric chair. Do they even do that anymore?

He's sitting there, looking at me—and then, he smiles. "Is everything okay?" he asks, still smiling. He stretches his long arms across the back of the couch, one on either side of himself, relaxing like he doesn't have a care in the world.

"Uh... nothing?"

He doesn't look like he's about to start choking. He doesn't look any different at all. Surely, Zelda couldn't have got away with selling poison all this while.

His eyebrows rise in a questioning way.

Right. He's probably not going to die on me. Time to move. I look like an idiot just standing here with a stupid look on my face. His dog breaks me from my stupor. Tyrion runs in circles around my ankles, probably smelling the coffee. Or my paralyzing fear.

Praying the potion is nothing more than very expensive colored water, I walk over to him. "Here you go." I hand over the coffee. "Can I bring you milk or sugar?"

"No, thanks. Black is fine," he says sipping the coffee, "The cake was great, by the way."

"Great," I choke out. I sit back down opposite, nibbling on my cupcake and studying his face for any signs. I remember the gypsy telling me how fast the effects start. But how fast did she mean? I can only pray that it's all bull-shit like Andrea says.

"Are you ok?" he asks.

Now, I realize I'm staring. "S-sure," I stammer. Are his eyes a little glazed?

One corner of his mouth quirks up in the most panty-melting smirk I've ever seen.

Holy. Moly. What is happening here? Is he flirting with me? No, he's just smiling. That's what it is. He can't help the fact that everything he does is sexy.

"You know something?" he continues with a gleam in his eye.

"What?" I breathe. No, I don't know anything right

now. Every thought, every sensation is all wrapped up in him.

I feel his foot brush against mine under the table. Stroking gently. My heartbeat quickens as my eyes meet his and he's looking at me in a way I've wanted him to for so long.

"I'm really glad you asked me over for dinner tonight."

I barely notice when he takes the cup from my hands—good thing, since I might have dropped it. I think shock is making my brain go haywire. "W-why are you so glad, then?" I whisper as my heart goes a mile a minute. Isn't it exactly what I want? Yes, but I'm afraid it might all be a dream. That it is just the work of the magic in the cupcake.

He stares deep into my eyes. "Because I might not have had the chance to see how gorgeous you are, otherwise. Always running in or out, always bundled up. I could hardly see you. I didn't get the opportunity to talk to you until now. I'm so glad I did, finally."

Gulp. "You are?"

He moves closer than ever, until I can feel the hard, unyielding thigh against mine. Our legs are actually touching. Oh, my goodness, it's been too long since I've had a man.

But then, I've never even been this close to a man like him.

"Yes. I am," he murmurs.

His breath is so warm and sweet on my face. I lick my lips. I swear it's a purely nervous gesture with nothing behind it, but he groans in the back of his throat.

It's working. Oh, my God, it's working. I can't believe how fast it is working! He's reaching out to tuck a strand of hair behind my ear. Even that simple, gentle touch sends a shiver down my spine.

"I can't believe how much I want to touch you," he

whispers, sounding genuinely surprised. I wonder what he'd think if I told him why the urge is suddenly so strong. No, I don't have to wonder. He'll be screaming abuse then out the door as fast as his big, masculine legs will go.

I feel his hands on my shoulders, kneading gently. Then his breath on my neck and he's kissing me. His lips feel so soft against my skin I gasp quietly. It feels unbelievably good. Divine, actually.

He takes my hand and we sit on the sofa together, smiling. I'm trying to play it cool but I haven't been in this situation for such a long time and I feel out of my depth. He's playing with my hands, stroking them, running his fingers through mine. Just the slightest touch from him sends electric shivers through my body.

His fingers trace the line of my jaw and I can hardly breathe. This is happening. This is really happening. The potion was real all along. It's completely illogical, but the proof is right here, leaning in, closing the distance between us, one breathless inch at a time until…

Until our mouths meet and I sink into the sweetest, deepest, most toe-curling kiss imaginable. He slides his hands into my hair, holding my head in place while his mouth moves sensuously over mine. I can barely bear it because so many things are hitting me at once.

He nibbles at my bottom lip and I feel his tongue against it, warm and soft. God, he's good at this. We're embracing, passionately, our arms wrapped around each other as we kiss even deeper. A feeling of unadulterated lust surges through my body, any insecurities from earlier is completely gone. I *do* still know how to do this I think to myself as his hands snake down my back, pulling me closer.

And oh my dear Lord—it's fucking great.

I run my hands up his back, feeling his muscular shoulders, his whole body so taut and firm through his T-shirt.

He unbuttons my shirt, kissing my exposed throat. His hands are around my waist. "God, you're beautiful," he murmurs, as his fingers reach for the first button on my shirt.

"So are you," I whisper back, my fingers creeping up inside his shirt and finally touching that gorgeous trail of hair, tracing it from his navel to the top of his jeans. I let my fingers trail further down, over the bulge of his pants and he quietly groans.

He kisses the silky skin of my breasts that are exposed. His hand cups them. He breaks off the kiss just long enough to smile, then wraps me up in another—even deeper—kiss that completely knocks my world off its axis. His tongue slides between my lips and touches mine as my fingers curl into claws that just about tear his T-shirt. And oh, jeez, his shoulders are even stronger than they look. I couldn't have imagined he would feel so good under my hands.

What feels even better is his hands and what they're doing to me. He strokes my hair, then trails down to my back. His fingers press and stroke, pulling me closer, working their way down to the hem of my blouse. When he touches the sensitive skin just above the waistband of my jeans, I arch my back and moan into his mouth.

This is really happening. I can't believe it, but here we are.

He pushes me back a little and I can't help but let him ease me against the couch cushions, one of my legs finding a way to wrap around his and pull him in. He kisses my cheek, my jaw, my ear. His breath is hot, fast and sends shivers down my spine. I hold onto the back of his neck before plunging both hands into his hair, holding his head in place as he nibbles my neck.

When I groan softly, he chuckles and does it again. A little harder this time. Playing with me. He's loving this as much as I am.

Oh, yes. Judging by the hardness pressing against my hip, he's *very* into this. I can't help but rub against it a little. He's not the only one who can play.

He then ups the ante by lifting my lace and satin camisole over my head, leaving my skin and the dancing nerves exposed. His hand slides over my stomach and up, cupping one of my breasts before moving even further to touch my face and sink into my hair again.

"I just wanna let you know something," I manage to breathe between kisses.

"Hmm?" he whispers in my ear.

"I don't usually do this on the first date."

His hands slide up and down my thighs and the heat growing between my legs gets hotter than ever. "Then you haven't had nearly enough fun in your life." He chuckles before slipping his tongue back into my mouth.

It is the sexiest thing anyone has done to me.

Knock, knock, knock.

We both freeze—my hand on his butt, his hand on my boob, staring at each other like a couple of teenagers who just got caught dry humping in Mom and Dad's rec room.

"I just won't answer," I whisper, straining upward for another kiss because I'm pretty sure I'll die if he doesn't kiss me again, right this very minute. It's like a thirst I didn't know I had until just now.

Funny how such intense thirst can disappear the second the sound of a key sliding into the lock hits my ears.

Chapter Fifteen

LAUREN

Only one person has a key to this apartment besides me, Danny, and the landlord. Considering the fact that the landlord doesn't even live in the city and he owes us twenty-four hours advance warning before paying a visit and Danny would boil himself to death rather than ruin my rare romantic interlude, it can only be only be one person on the other side of that door.

Only one person I know who's obnoxious enough and clueless enough to try to walk into my house without announcement. Only one terrible person I'm stupid enough to have given a key to, but only under strict assurance that it would be used in case of emergency and for no other reason.

My mother.

"Oh shit," I hiss, leaping away from Jackson.

"Who is that?" Jackson asks from the couch.

I want to die. I want to literally drop dead on this very spot. "My mom," I mutter, as I pull my camisole back on, and dash to the door, and throw myself against it to get the chain latch in place before the key can do its job.

I can't imagine what Jackson must be thinking. Yeah, I guess I forgot to mention when describing her that she doesn't just bake well. She's also an expert at killing the mood, butting in where she doesn't belong and inserting herself into situations which have nothing to do with her.

"Lauren? Sweetheart? Why can't I get the door open? And why is it so dark in there?"

This can't be happening. It's a nightmare. It's got to be. I'm half-undressed, flushed and breathless with two dogs running circles around me, barking their little heads off. I pat down my hair, trying to compose myself and open the door as far as the chain will allow.

I peer out through the gap. I'm annoyed, but I don't want to upset my mother. "Mom, what are you doing here? You know I gave you that key for emergencies."

"I'm sorry, darling. I didn't think you'd mind. I wanted to know how you got on with your sister and since you've been busy recently, I decided to make a batch of your favorite red velvet cupcakes and bring it over." And damned if she's not carrying a Tupperware cake saver full of red velvet cupcakes.

I exhale. It is almost useless trying to talk to my mother. "Didn't you get my text?"

"Oh," she says blankly, "I don't think I did. Was it something important?"

"Uh, Mom… now's not the best time for you to come in."

"What? Are you locking the door against your own mother?"

"Of course not, but I have company," I announce, standing between her and the rest of the house. The dogs are going nuts now, probably because they can smell the sweets my mother's carrying. Draco tries to wriggle his way out through the gap in the door.

"No, Draco!" I bend down to grab him before he can run out into the hall, and Tyrion buries his nose between my boobs. Oh, my God, this is madness.

"Would you just let me in already? I won't stay long and Draco obviously wants to see me even if you don't," she sniffs in that voice that is designed to make me feel guilty. "And since when do you have a second dog? Do I have a new grand-puppy you didn't tell me about?"

I hate it when she treats Draco like her grandkid—a not-so-subtle reminder of the fact that I'm childless, like being single in my mid-twenties is a crime. "He isn't mine," I bite out as I get the dogs under control. "Here. Just come in, I guess."

She's already practically sticking her face through the opening, anyway. She breezes into the house the moment I get the chain off the door.

"So why didn't you call first?"

"I tried to call, sweetheart, but you didn't answer."

I find that hard to believe—or maybe she's telling the truth, since I've been a little too wrapped up in my guest to notice anything like the phone.

"Oh. Well. That still doesn't mean you can just show up and use the key," I complain when we reach the kitchen, where she leaves the carrier of cupcakes on the counter.

She takes in my state of undress with one quick glance, sighing and shaking her head. "I'll never understand fashion nowadays," she grumbles. "Look at you. You're practically undressed, and with company. In my day that would have been considered underwear."

"Mom, stop, please," I whisper with my cheeks burning

like they're on fire. I can just imagine what Jackson must be thinking. "This is... the new style."

"It's very pretty though. And very flattering. Where did you buy it from?"

Oh Jeez, give it a rest! She's got a twinkle in her eye and I can't tell if she's just winding me up. "I can't remember, really, I bought it ages ago." I'm not going to tell her it's from Victoria's Secret.

She unwinds the scarf from around her neck and my heart sinks because this means she thinks she's sticking around. I do not want her to stick around.

"And who's this?" she demands, her eyes lighting up as she spots Jackson on the sofa.

He's sitting there clutching a cushion to his lap.

I just about manage to stifle a giggle. My heart is still racing. "This is Jackson," I say, "He's my neighbor. He— um, just came over for dinner."

"It's lovely to meet you!" she gushes.

"It's good to meet you too, Mrs. Appleton," he says, all charm and warmth now that his erection has gone down. "I understand you're an accomplished baker."

Boy, does he know just the right thing to say. She just about melts with pleasure—and I could kiss him for being so thoughtful. Or just in general, because I'd kiss him again for pretty much any reason because whoa—the man can kiss.

"Why, I am. I see my daughter's been bragging about me." She beams in my general direction.

I can only shrug with a grin.

"And if your red velvet cupcakes are any indication, I can see why," he adds. He's really laying on the charm thick. Like with a trowel.

Meanwhile, I'm biting the side of my tongue to keep from laughing hysterically. This is all a joke, right? It has to be. He's praising my mother's cupcakes when I slipped a freaking potion into his, while I'm standing here half-undressed with a dog that won't stop trying to hump my damn leg.

Mom doesn't notice my discomfort. She's too involved with eating up the attention—to the point where she hurries into the kitchen and comes back with another cupcake from the batch she brought. "I keep telling Lauren that she should find a nice man like you. Are you single?"

I nearly die in horror. Will the humiliation ever stop? Has anyone ever died from it?

This really should be enough to negate any effect of the magic potion. It is certainly enough to cause Jackson to remove the cushion from his crotch and stand. "Yes, I am," he confirms.

"Mom you should go," I say quickly.

"Yes, yes, I don't want to interrupt you young people, but maybe I can persuade your new..." She pauses and I give her a look. "...friend," she says.

I breathe a sigh of relief.

"To try one of my red velvet cupcakes."

"Um...no. I'd better be going," Jackson says instantly.

"Oh, I hope I didn't interrupt your nice evening!" Mom says. "Please don't go because of me. I can put the kettle on and we can all have a cup of tea if you like? Keep you warm Lauren in that little top of yours."

I'm pretty much dying of embarrassment as the situation sinks in. I'm standing here in my underwear with my gorgeous neighbor who I couldn't believe even agreed to come over. I've given him some strange potion that I have no idea is even safe! And my Mom is here!!

"I really need to go," Jackson says, "But thank you so much for dinner and everything." He smiles and kisses me on the cheek.

"You're welcome." What else can I say? Mom's still standing right here in the room with us.

"Goodbye, Mrs. Appleton," he says, offering his hand to Mom.

"Sally! Just call me Sally." Ignoring his hand, she throws her tentacles around him in a bear hug.

As soon, she removes them he practically runs out of my house.

Great! I guess I'm not the first person to ever be cock-blocked by my mother.

Chapter Sixteen

LAUREN

I took Danny's advice and walked into the office with my head held up high. At first, I could feel people staring at me, then as the morning went on and I went about my business as if nothing was amiss they started looking at me with a mixture of confusion and astonishment. Was I too stupid to realize how monumental my screw up was, or did I know something they didn't.

I enjoyed the feeling of having confounded them.

"You're never going to believe this," I say to Nina over my cell phone. My eyes dart from side to side as I huddle over my desk.

"What happened? Oh, my God, did you use the potion? I knew you would. What happened?"

"Could you let me talk? How can I get to the juicy stuff if you won't let me get a word in?"

"Sorry, sorry. Hurry up."

"I didn't use the potion, but Danny did," I whisper.

"He did what?" she screams in my ear.

"He realized he had done wrong and apologized," I

add quickly. I don't want Nina to hate Danny. That would never do because I love them both.

"And he ate it?"

"Every bite. There were hardly any crumbs left, even." I can't help but smile as I do, even though I feel more than a little wicked when I think about it.

"And? Did anything happen?"

"You could say that…" I trail off with a giggle.

"Oh, my God, I swear, I'm gonna come there and kill you if you don't stop playing games and tell me everything."

"We maybe made out. A lot."

Her squeal is ear-splitting. "I'm so happy. I'm so happy I hate you a little but I'm so happy!"

I cover my mouth to quiet my laugh so no one else hears. "It was amazing, Nina."

"You stopped at making out, though?" she asks, and she doesn't sound like she believes me.

"I did, but even if we didn't, so what?"

"I was just wondering. The way you describe him, I'm not sure I could've stopped at just making out, is all."

Memories from last night flash back in my mind when she says that. Oh, who am I kidding? I haven't been able to top thinking about it. It's amazing that I even managed to get out of bed this morning. I almost forgot to feed the dog. I was that out of it.

"Between you and me? I probably wouldn't have stopped if we weren't interrupted by my mother."

"Your mother? No effing way," she hisses.

"Yes, effing way…and believe me, we had a long talk once he left. All about boundaries. I might have eaten maybe five red velvet cupcakes that I detest after she left, I was so stressed out. And the punchline is, we'll just end up having the same conversation the next time she does it again."

"You poor thing." Nina sighs.

"I wanted to go over and apologize to him, but I didn't want to come off as being too clingy or like I was over-thinking what happened before Mom showed up. You know? I want him to think I'm cool."

"But you're not cool."

"I know, but is it so bad to want him to think so?"

"Hey, how do you know the potion worked and it was just not natural? Like maybe he really wanted you anyway and the potion had nothing to do with it."

"It had to be the potion."

"Why?" she asks.

"Well, I guess because it was so sudden. He was actually yawning and asking for coffee to keep awake, then he eats the cupcake, and suddenly he's fully awake and can't get enough of me. I'd call that a pretty abrupt change of heart. Actually, I still can't believe how fast it worked!"

"Right," she says slowly. "I guess in a way that sucks, but hey!" she continues, and there's sunshine in her voice again. "That means last night wasn't the only chance you'll get. I mean, the world is your oyster now. I bet he'd have thought you were cool even if you went over last night to pick up where you left off. You don't have to follow the whole three-day rule thingy. You can break all the rules now. Oh, my God, just think. You can do anything you want, and he will still want you desperately!"

"I don't know about that," I fret in a tight whisper. At the back of my mind, something niggles. *You didn't get him fair and square. You'll never know whether he would have wanted you without the potion. Damn you Danny for taking that away from me.*

"It's magic, babe. He'll be like your fuck-slave from now on," she says cheerfully.

I frown. "I meant, who knows how long this is going to last?"

"You're impossible. Did I ever tell you that?" she growls.

"What?"

"I'm just saying, why don't you try being happy that things went great and he was super into you? I mean, what's the point of always looking at the negative side of things? I don't know if it lasts forever, but it lasted for the girl I told you about."

"Hmm. And do you think it eventually turns into, you know, real love?"

The line goes quiet and I'm about to say something else, to dismiss my silly question.

Nina gets there first, "I don't know what you mean," she says in a confused voice. And then, "Of course it's real love, silly. What other kind is there?"

"The kind that only happens when you take a potion."

There's silence again and I feel like I should be having this conversation with Danny, not Nina. "Right, I better get going. Thanks for the chat."

"No worries, babe," she replies, back to her chirpy self. "And chill. I just know he'll be aching to ask you out after that steamy kiss you told me about."

I smile and hang up. I go to the vending machine. Get myself a bar of chocolate. Walk back to my desk.

The little ringer symbol flashes silent on my phone and I slip it into my handbag, vowing to myself that I won't look at it until the end of the day.

I savor each mouthful of dark chocolate as I shut off the critical voice in my head and let my imagination take me on a trip back to the previous evening... and what might have happened if Mom hadn't come back. I think

about the warm smoothness of his tanned skin against my
fingertips.

Chapter Seventeen

LAUREN

My heart thuds like a bass drum as I walk toward my front door. Is he home yet? Probably not. He has his own firm, after all. When I look back, I don't remember ever hearing him get home before seven or eight o'clock.

It makes me wonder if I should offer to walk Tyrion for him. Poor guy probably hates being left alone until all hours, and he did seem to like me last night. Maybe even a little too much.

I notice the note on my door right away. It's the sort of thing that sticks out. My hand shakes as I reach for it. I pull it from the door and unfold it.

Movie tonight? 7:30?

Under that, two boxes. One's labeled *Yes* and the other, much smaller, almost minuscule box is labeled *No*.

My heart soars.

Is it possible that he really thinks I'd say no? Evidently not, seeing as how he barely gave me the space to reject him. I giggle all the way through finding a pen in my purse, through making an X through the *Yes* box, and sliding the note under his door.

I love his sense of humor.

It isn't until I'm leashing up Draco that doubt starts creeping up on me again like the pesky five pounds I'm always trying to get rid of for good. I can't shake it, no matter how completely out of my mind with happiness I am at the thought of Jackson wanting to see me again.

THIS ISN'T FAIR TO HIM.

Damn it, I wish I had never bought that love potion. It's heavy guilt too, the sort that makes me drag my feet along the sidewalk even as Draco prances around in front of me.

He has no idea why he likes me so much, and that's unfair to a nice guy like him.

I should tell him.

But if I tell him, he won't want to be around me anymore. I don't know if I could handle that. Besides, he's a terrific guy and not just the gorgeous heartthrob I already knew he was when I visited Zelda. Now I know why she was so unhappy when I admitted to not knowing Jackson. What if I had slipped him the potion without knowing anything about him, and he'd turned out to be a real asshole? I could have sentenced myself to life with a wacko. So yeah, I got lucky.

Now that I know it works, and how fast it works, the thought of how bad this could've turned out chills me even more than the cool, late-winter breeze.

That doesn't make me feel any better though. If anything, it makes me feel worse. Because in this scenario, I'm the wacko. I bought a love potion! This is the 21st century. Who does that?

But hey—who's to say he won't fall for you for real? You're not exactly a monster.

I feel so confused, and slightly depressed. Nina would slap me upside the head if she could hear my thoughts right now. But I can't help it. I'm not Nina.

Draco looks up at me at just that moment, like he can read my thoughts. "Well, I'm not," I whisper as we continue our walk. Jackson could do much, much worse than me. I'm not clingy, I'm not vapid. I'm a darn good cook, I love to read and my musical tastes are vast. I would never begrudge a boyfriend his time with the guys, just like I would expect him to encourage my girl time.

I'm a catch, damn it. He could do a hell of a lot worse.

So I'm not going to feel bad for him.

And I'm not going to blame myself, either. I didn't use the potion. Danny did. Besides, I would be a terrific girlfriend for him. The best. Eating that cupcake might just be the luckiest thing he's ever done.

I just wish my heart didn't ache when I think that. I can imagine people asking us years from now how we met. Sure, we're next-door neighbors, so I could always use that as my explanation and it wouldn't be a lie.

But I would know, deep down inside, that it was more than that. How long could I handle the truth weighing on me?

I'm afraid I bought a lot more than just a love potion from a gypsy named Zelda.

Chapter Eighteen

JACKSON

I can't believe I'm this excited to take a girl to the movies. Who am I?

Tyrion's picking up the vibes off me and bouncing off the walls.

"Calm down, would you?" I say after I almost trip over him on the way to the door. "Anyone would think you were the one with a date tonight. And don't try breaking out to visit Draco, either." Okay. I am, talking to the dog like he's a person. What's going on with me? I think I'm happy.

I'm definitely the guy who wants to see a woman two nights in a row, which is something I never could've been accused of in the past. I normally hold women at arm's length for the first three, four, five dates. Depending on how busy I am and how interesting she is.

But Lauren.

Lauren's different.

I can't describe it, but it's something I feel inside, and I know how stupid that sounds because I just met the woman. It sounds stupid enough even in my own mind, but there it is. I can't deny it. There's something different about her.

She's...effortless.

With her, I don't have to try. I can have a conversation with her. There's a refreshing honesty about her. She's natural. And she's warm. And kind. And she even puts up with that piece of work mother of hers. She's a sly one, but pretends to be a bumbling fool. Which earns Lauren a spot in Heaven if there is such a place. I sure as hell couldn't handle her with so much grace on the regular.

The memory of her arrival, of how awkward and poorly timed the whole situation was, is enough for me to make certain the next time will be at my place. I suppose it was a good thing she showed up just when she did.

I lost my senses last night.

Sex after one dinner with my next-door neighbor? That's not me, a little too much like begging for trouble. If it were terrible, there would be no avoiding her afterward. Never spit in your own rice bowl, my grandfather used to say.

Still, I was going to. I was more than ready to.

I have to be smarter than that tonight, is all. I want to get to know this girl, but I can't let myself get swept up. *Keep your cool, man.* I straighten my shirt collar.

Chapter Nineteen

LAUREN

"So, tonight's the night then!" Danny yells as the front door bangs shut behind him.

I walk out of my room to greet him. "I thought you were coming home early to help me get ready!"

He takes his hat off and holds it in his hand as he scans his eyes over me. "Turn around," he orders.

I obey.

He straightens the collar of my top slightly and tucks my hair behind my ear. "You look stunning," he tells me, grinning. "You didn't need my help, after all. And yeah, sorry, got caught up at work, you know."

I chew at my lip. "Do you *really* think I look ok?"

"You look great, but…"

"But?"

He looks thoughtful for a moment, and then the twinkle comes back to his eyes. "I thought you'd be wearing your new top?" he asks with mock confusion, "You know the one your Mom liked so much?"

"Shut up," I tell him sternly.

He moves his face closer to mine and peers at me.

"What?" I ask worriedly.

"What have you done with your eyes? They look amazing."

"I followed an online tutorial," I reply, feeling pleased with myself. I wasn't usually one to wear a great deal of makeup but Jackson was certainly worth the extra effort.

He lifts me up by my hips and swings me around, making me feel even giddier than I already do. "You look like a million dollars, baby girl. Now go get him!" he says setting me down.

"He's picking me up here, actually." I glance at my watch.

Danny laughs. "Ah, yes, the convenience of dating your neighbor. I wonder if you'll make it back here tonight... or you will be busy *not* sleeping next door."

"Oi," I tell him, pointing a warning finger at him, "I'll be in my own bed, you'll see. We're just going to the movies. It's just going to be a nice chilled date. No naughtiness. No Mom either!"

There's a knock at the door and I freeze.

"I'll get it," he says.

I nervously take a last look in the mirror. My eyes do look nice, I think. I hope. The green brings out the green flecks in my hazel eyes and compliments the pale green silk top I'm wearing. I've gone for black jeans and high-heeled knee length boots. He's so tall I felt I could do with the extra height. I hear them introducing themselves to each other.

I take a deep breath.

"Hey!" he says, smiling as he walks in beside Danny. Next to Danny, who is no lightweight in the looks department, he *is* an unbelievably gorgeous specimen of a man. I can't imagine ever getting tired of just gazing at him. To my surprise, he looks a little bit in awe at the sight of me too. He's looking at me as if I am beautiful. The way men look at Nina. God, how I wish I knew whether it was just the potion or if it's real.

He comes forward and stops in front of me. He's freshly shaved, his jawline smooth and perfect. Green eyes twinkling and dimples creasing. And he smells delicious. "You look beautiful," he whispers.

I think I might faint. "Umm…you don't look too bad yourself."

He grins. "Shall we go?"

"Nice to meet you, Jackson," Danny yells as we leave together. "And have a great night, you guys. I won't wait up for you, Lolly!"

Ugh. Really? I give him a look as I close the door behind me.

"Lolly?" Jackson teases, as we walk down the steps towards his car.

"It's an old nickname," I tell him. "My friend Nina started it and it kind of just stuck. With some people, anyway."

He laughs. "I think it's cute. Should I call you that too?"

"If you really want to," I say, rolling my eyes. "But just don't introduce me to your parents like that!" My stomach lurches. What the hell did I say that for? "Not that I'm expecting to meet your parents, or anything!" I quickly add.

"Oh, I don't know, I met your Mom on our first date, so maybe I should get you back," he replies, grinning at me and…winking.

Oh, my Lord! This man can actually make my knees tremble.

"So, you're not very keen on Lolly, then? Maybe I'll have to think of a new nickname for you."

We're in a cab heading to the movie theatre and I'm thinking about how much I would love for him to have a nickname for me. "If you want," I whisper.

He look deep into my eyes and for a while, it feels as if there is no one else in the universe except the two of us ensconced in this warm taxi and hurtling through the stars in space. Then he lifts a finger and touches my bottom lip. "Are you real?" he murmurs, his voice full with wonder.

A cold claw clutches my stomach making me shudder. All this is because of the potion. None of it is real.

"Are you okay?" he asks, a frown beginning to form on his forehead.

I quickly nod and force a smile. "So what are we watching?"

He smiles. "How do you feel about horror movies?" he asks me tentatively.

"I love them!" I lie. I don't really like slasher movies at all. Give me a romantic comedy any day, but I really don't care what movie we see. I just want to sit in the darkness with him.

"Great. There's a new one out. A remake of The Ring. It's meant to be really scary. You know, the one where the girl crawls out of the TV screen?"

I have no idea, but I just nod and smile, and try not to think about creepy girls crawling out of TVs.

Our seats are at the back of the mostly empty movie theatre and we settle into an empty row with our salty popcorn and huge cups of Mountain Dew. I wonder if he picked the back-row seats on purpose. I sneak a look at him, his profile gives nothing away. I haven't made out in the back row of the movies in forever. .

"How was work today?" I ask him, but the movie is starting.

He leans over and whispers in my ear, "Terrible." Then he smiles. "But I'm with you now."

My stomach flutters and when I lean back I realize his arm is around me, so I slant into him instead and pray that he can't hear my heart which is thumping loud and fast.

It's soon thumping for a different reason though and when I let out a loud gasp, my hands flying to cover my mouth, he chuckles and pulls me in closer.

"I thought you liked horror movies," he whispers, smirking at me, but in a kind way.

I like when you whisper like that in my ear, I think to myself, breathing in his musky aftershave. "I do," I whisper back in protest. "I just didn't realize this one was going to be so scary."

"That's generally the idea," he replies, still looking amused, and then he takes my hand and puts it on his arm. The girth of his bicep is impressive and his skin is so smooth and taut. "Just squeeze tight if you need to," he tells me.

"Ok." I smile, trying to look normal even though my retinas are scarred with the bone-chilling images I've just seen. I hope I don't have nightmares tonight! I adjust my eyes to just below the screen, letting them glaze over, blissfully out of focus, breathing slow and deep.

It's not until about halfway through and a particularly blood-curdling scream that my eyes flick back to the screen and I witness the gore and horror. My fingers close tightly around Jackson's beautiful bicep, squeezing, pushing the awful images from my mind. I don't even realize I'm closing my eyes, until I feel his soft lips meet with mine. I blink them open quickly and then shut again.

He's kissing me. Oh, yes. That's better. It feels so good.

I kiss him back, my hand still gripped tight around his

bicep. I love the way I can feel his muscles flex slightly with his every tiny movement.

His tongue enters my mouth, or does mine search for his first? I feel myself sinking into a safe haven of pleasure, the screams onscreen no longer bother me as his arms hug me tight.

I feel his hand on my throat, stroking, moving up to my face and then his thumb in my mouth as his kisses follow down my neck. I suck on his thumb, biting it gently and now his other hand is on my breast, squeezing softly, finding the erect mound of my nipple and pinching.

My hands are all over him, feeling his chest, his back, his glorious arms, and I'm clawing at him, needing to feel all him at once, wanting him.

His fingertips snake down my belly and pop open the button on my jeans and—oh god, I want to feel his touch down there. His fingertips brushing against my stomach softly, making me want him more and more.

I glance around quickly at the sound of another scream, brought back to reality momentarily, but there is no-one else around us and getting naughty with Jackson is a million times more preferable than watching the movie.

"Relax," he whispers, smiling, kissing me, gently and then more urgently, as his hand ventures further down and into my lace panties. His fingertips glide over me and find exactly the right place and I moan into his mouth as he rubs me.

Oh, wow!

His hands push my legs wider, then he lightly brushes against my slit. I widen my legs automatically. I am so wet he growls deep in his throat as his fingers plunges in. His thumb rubs against my clit as his finger moves in and out, all the while his mouth is on mine, our tongues entwined.

His breath is heavy, almost panting, and I love how much he desires me. I want it to last forever.

He withdraws his hand, and in my head, I'm screaming No, don't you dare. I'm so close to climax.

In the darkness, his eyes gleam. "I'm dying for a taste of Appleton pie," he drawls as he yanks my jeans and panties right down to my knees.

I gasp in shock. Jesus!

Surely, he's not intending to…

"You're a bad, bad girl, Miss Appleton," he whispers wickedly.

Before I know it, his head is in my lap, his tongue straining to reach me. The delicate flicks from the tip of his tongue make me cry out just like one of the poor desperate victims in the movie. I lean back in my chair and pull his beautiful head closer so his tongue can get even deeper as he hungrily licks my pussy. Oh, my God, the licking this man does. Like he can't get enough. Like I'm the sweetest, most delicious thing, he ever tasted.

I never knew it could be like this. His dedication is astounding. He misses nothing. Every fold, every crease is seen to lovingly, lingeringly. It's like his tongue is saying, mine, mine, mine. High-octane waves of rapture start flowing through my veins.

He takes my clit between his lips and simultaneously jams two fingers into me. I grind my ass up and down as he begins to finger fuck me furiously. I have to cap my hand over my mouth to muffle the moans as waves of intense pleasure cascade through me. "Holy shit," I whisper, my hips jerking faster than ever. "Oh, Jackson, I'm gonna…!" I've never come so fast in my whole life.

Damn!

I'd stepped into the beginning of a climax that stripped me of all reason, but Jackson just keeps on going and I just keep on coming. The convulsions take a long time to subside. My heart beat races and I pant hard. Thank God, it's dark in here, and thank God everybody else is too busy paying attention to the movie to notice me coming in the back row.

I stare at the screen blankly as Jackson eagerly laps up the juices that came out of my pussy and flooded his face as if it is the sweetest wine. It feels like the most natural thing in the world to have his tongue licking between my legs.

Chapter Twenty

JACKSON

"You should have told me you don't like horror movies," I tell her as we walk down the street. Her cheeks are burning like her whole face is about to burst into flame.

"Yeah, I'm the type that screams and ducks down to avoid looking at the screen, but you know what? I think I really like them now." She gives me a teasing smile.

Her eyes are bright and sparkling and I stare at her in awe. I've never felt like this about any woman before. I used to laugh at my friends for acting like love-sick pussies and now I'm doing the same. I put my arm around her and catch another whiff of her shampoo. It hints of lime and coconut. I can't believe it but I'm rock-hard without her having to do anything but rest against me.

What the hell?

I brush my mouth against her forehead and relish the softness of her skin. There's something seriously sexy about this woman. She's gorgeous but she acts like she isn't, for a start. She goes to my head like a glass of champagne, the way the old song says. I never quite understood that until just now. I feel dizzy, foggy, like I would if I were half-drunk. I might as well be, only it's her I'm drunk on. And making her come like that in the movie theatre. No woman has had that effect on me. I can't keep my hands off her.

I love how she just let herself go like that. I can't remember the last time I did anything so risqué in public; it's not usually my thing. But tonight I didn't have a choice. I could fucking smell her arousal and I *had* to taste her, or I would have gone raving crazy in that cinema. It had been seriously hot though, and I'm still buzzing from it.

"I enjoyed watching you scream," I say with a wink.

She blushes bright red.

Damned if that doesn't turn me on.

"No offense, but I think there would have been way more screams if I'd had to actually watch the whole thing!" she says.

My eyebrows rise. "Is that a challenge?"

She gives me a look, full of daring. "Maybe."

I don't know if she's trying to be seductive or not, but fuck it, it definitely has me all wired up. "You're on." I glance at the time. It's just 10:00. Time enough for one drink. "I know this great little place around here that does out of this world cocktails. Feel like having one?"

"Well, I can't say no to out of this world cocktails," she says, slipping her arm through mine.

Work has kept me busy and I haven't been there for a while, but when we arrive, the cocktail list is still impressive.

"This is nice," she murmurs, looking around, "How did you find it?"

"I used to come here with my grandfather," I tell her. "He lived in a care home nearby and we used to sneak out and drink cocktails here."

"That's so adorable," she gushes, smiling that unashamed smile of hers that makes me smile too.

I'd deliberately chosen the example I knew would make her heart melt. Telling her I'd brought numerous girls here probably wouldn't have gone down so well, not that she needed to worry. None of them had anything on her. But that was all a while ago now anyway, the days before when I was a carefree young man.

In truth, it had only been on one occasion that I'd been here with Gramps, when he was still around. But the memory was so vivid it could have been a hundred times. The bartender had laughed at the sight of an old man in a hospital gown and a scruffy student sitting together drinking cosmos in the middle of the afternoon and the thought still makes me smile. We'd felt like naughty children sitting there, drinking in a bar, breaking the care home rules. It was one of the last afternoons spent together before the cancer finally got the better of him.

She's perusing the cocktail list, biting her bottom lip, which is the sexiest thing ever and I feel a stirring in my pants. It's incredible how much this girl turns me on. I almost feel out of control. "Anything take your fancy?" I ask her.

"I always go for the same thing." She hands the menu to me. "Why don't you surprise me?"

I order us two cosmopolitans. It's what Gramps and I had, all those years before.

"This is great," she says, taking a sip.

Her eyes look so beautiful tonight. So sparkly. I could look at her forever. Jeez, what's happening to me!? "Oh. Um…" And since when do I trip over my tongue like this? "So tell me about what you do, then. I know hardly anything about you." Totally bizarre, but I actually *want* to hear everything about the woman I'm dating.

She hesitates and crinkles up her cute little nose before telling me about an amusingly bad day in her life. She screws up her nose again. "It's so frustrating because I know our system is the best out there and I wish my colleagues would recognize that ."

"For what it's worth, I agree with Danny. If it were my company, I would only give the job to the company most qualified and with the best solution to my problem. A shoe landing on my face would not affect my decision."

"I really hope Danny and you are right," she says, sipping her cocktail and looking straight at me.

It's weird and beautiful and maybe I'm quietly going totally crazy here, but the way she looks at me with that vulnerable, open expression, makes me feel as if I can see straight into her soul. I'm trying to concentrate on what she's saying...

I nod and hold her hand, I love watching her talk. Her eyes twinkle and she's so expressive, gesturing wildly with her other hand.

"I'm finished. Next drinks are on me."

Before I can act macho and tell her I'll get it, she is already up and away. I watch her walk to the bar, her hips slender and shapely in black jeans. Her hair long, so shiny and glossy, swishing against her back as she moves. My head might be scrambled with work and trying to get my apartment finished, but I have to admit to myself that the only thing I really care about at the moment… is her.

She comes back and as she settles my drink in front of me, I get another whiff of her hair. And my dick is instantly hard again. What did they make her shampoo with? Sex hormones?

"What is it?" she asks, looking at me with wide, innocent eyes.

She has no idea where my thoughts are, of course. My

filthy, filthy thoughts. If she did, she'd probably barricade herself in her house and call the cops. Oh, but the things I could do to this woman.

I grin, and I can't help how wolfish it is. "Would you believe I'm ready for more Appleton pie?"

The way her cheeks become rosy is just beautiful.

Chapter Twenty-One

LAUREN

He places two sliders on my plate, while I give him more than half of my fries. Just like I thought…we don't have to talk about it. Like we've known each other for years.

Jackson takes a bite of his mini burger. "Mmm. This is awesome."

"Not the healthy food I would've imagined you ordering," I point out with an arched eyebrow.

"Do you think a man wants to order a salad after watching a classic horror movie?" he asks.

I have to stop myself before I remind him that he hardly watched any of it. "A genre-defining one, no less." I smirk instead.

"Exactly, smartass. I don't want you thinking I'm some sort of health nut, either." He shoves a few fries into his mouth at once, like he's trying to prove his point.

"There's nothing wrong with being a health nut." But I'd never be one myself, and I can't imagine ever being one. Or being with one. It would get boring, I think, when

I'm not super into cross training or veganism or any of that.

"I still don't want you to get the wrong idea. Like I said last night, it's all about balance. I ate like a pig last night, so I spent an extra twenty at the gym today—and believe me, I struggled through it," he grimaces.

"Oh, I'm sorry."

"What are you apologizing for? I'm the one who went for seconds—I mean, granted, I wouldn't have if you weren't such an amazing cook, but I can hardly blame you for that." His eyes twinkle.

"It would be like blaming me for having brown hair. I just can't help it."

His laugh rings out over the conversation around us, and my heart just about bursts. I love making him laugh. I'd stand on my head for the rest of the night if he would just keep laughing like that.

"I happen to be a man who likes to eat." He's smirking behind the rim of his glass, so he knows what he said and how I could take it one of two ways.

Absolutely wicked. My body responds at the mere suggestion.

I need another sip of beer before I can speak above a broken whisper, "I-I think we'll get along very well, then— so long as it's not brains you're hungry for," I add, thinking back to the movie.

"No," he murmurs, still smirking. "It's not brains. You don't have to worry about that."

How is it humanly possible for one man to be so sexy? It's enough to make me forget to breathe, I swear. He just exudes it. His charm, the way he smiles, the way his voice lowers into a near growl—I'm surprised my panties haven't melted off.

And I'm not the only one who thinks so. A high-pitched giggle from the bar catches my attention and I glance over purely out of reflex, because when something catches your attention you look, right?

It's a trio of blondes who all look like they're taking the night off from being supermodels. Awesome. Just what I was hoping to see. Just the thing to make me feel really good about myself.

And they want his attention. They want it bad. All three of them keep trying to catch Jackson's eye, but he either doesn't notice or doesn't care.

Finally, just as he's draining the last of his beer, one of them slides off her stool and walks over. She's a little unsteady – had a bit to much to drink, I guess – and drunk girls always have more confidence. Or so I've noticed.

Sometimes, drunk girls even buy love potions.

"Excuse me." Blondie ignores me entirely, focusing on Jackson. "Have we met before? I think we've met before. At a party at Pete's?" She leans down a little, so her boobs can peak out of her V-neck sweater.

I wonder how she'd feel if I punched one of them.

I look at him, holding my breath to see how he'll respond.

He blinks, looking at her, then frowns a little. "Oh. Sure. Sorry, his parties are always so crowded."

She beams. "They are, aren't they? I was hoping to see you again, but you haven't been around." She bites down ever so slightly on her bottom lip, hopeful. Teasing him.

She sure wouldn't look so pretty if I pulled her teeth out, would she? I'm not normally this violent, but it takes a certain level of bitchiness to walk straight up to a guy who's clearly with another woman and pretend that woman doesn't exist. This place isn't even nearly crowded enough to pass that off as a mere accident.

He smiles again, and I can tell he's flattered.

Well, damn, it was fun while it lasted. Why would he want to hang around with me when he's got nearly six feet of perfect Nordic beauty—and her boobs—in his face?

"Yes, well, I've been busy. It's nice to see you again, though." He turns his focus to me. "You ready?"

Oh. I guess I am. Not that I have any beer or food left. It just seems sort of abrupt. I'm not complaining, however. Especially when Blondie falls back a little with her glossy lips in a pout. Poor thing.

I make it a point to smile at her as we're leaving—I mean, she looks so disappointed, I just want to bring her spirits up a little. She and her girlfriends want to spit nails, I can just tell. Maybe they should try not being so sleazy and obvious next time.

He gave her the brush-off in favor of me. Me! Hot damn!

"Why are you so smiley?" he asks as we step out into the cold.

I can't believe him. I really can't. "You didn't notice what just went on in there? Are you really that oblivious?"

"Ouch," he murmurs with a smirk. "Yeah, I noticed what was going on, but it was nothing."

"Yeah. I guess you're used to random bombshells throwing themselves at you wherever you go."

He stops, taking me by the hand and pulling me closer. "Hey. Wait a second. I want to make something clear."

I look up at him and get a little lost in those eyes of his. They're gorgeous—and intense, staring into mine. He means business right now. "What is it?"

"I'm out with you because I want to be with you," he murmurs, locking his fingers with mine. "You're the woman I'm out with tonight, and I wouldn't have it any other way. As far as I'm concerned, you're the only woman in the world."

I'm dreaming. I must be dreaming. But his kiss isn't a dream—firm, warm, tantalizing. The arm around my waist isn't a dream, holding me in a vice grip against his body. It's all very real.

I can hardly hear the traffic rushing past us for the rush of blood in my ears, creating a storm in my head. He wants me. He really wants me. And damn... if I don't want him more every minute we spend together.

"Let's go home," he whispers when the kiss ends, our foreheads touching as our breath creates a fog around our heads.

"Yes. Let's," I agree, ready to flag the first cab I see.

Chapter Twenty-Two

LAUREN

I'm still on cloud nine from the movies, my head a little light-headed from the two cosmopolitans. It makes it easier to ignore the fact that it must be the love potion that made him act so crazy. To get me off in public with his mouth when we hardly know each other? I mean, that's sort of a big deal. Whatever Zelda sold me must've been the Extra Strength version. No wonder it was so expensive.

I don't think twice about accepting his invitation of a night cap. I'm curious to see the inside of his place. That's what I tell myself, but obviously, I'm a flesh and blood human being, and he did mention something about being ready for more Appleton pie.

"Whisky?" he asks while I scratch Tyrion's stomach.

I screw up my nose.

"Baileys?"

"Mmmm, yes please. On the rocks."

"Coming right up."

I look around me curiously. "It all looks new. I wish our

place was so polished and minimalistic," I say with a hint of envy.

He comes back into view holding a dog biscuit. Tyrion jumps up and runs to him. "To be honest, I prefer your place. It feels like more like a home."

"Aw thanks," I say. "But it does get messy with Draco, sometimes though. His fur gets everywhere!"

"Don't I know it? I have the same problem."

I take a seat on his huge leather sofa and look around while he fixes the drinks. There's a selection of hardback books on his pristine glass coffee table and I look to see what he has. One about sailing, another entitled, 'Modern architecture: A photographic history.' That makes sense. There's another about architecture but without pictures and then I let out a squeal when I come to the last in the pile. "The Magic of Harry Potter."

"Find something you like?" he asks, smiling as he comes back with the drinks.

I hold up the book to show him. "It's my favorite film of all time!" I practically shriek, clasping my hands together in excitement. And then I shut up and sip on my drink as I remember Nina's advice and that I'm not meant to act too keen. So many rules to the dating game, according to her. And apparently disobeying them could affect my whole future!

When he opens a cupboard, and digs out a CD of the movie it's all I can do to stop myself proposing to him right there and then. But...Nina advice is very firm in my head.

"I can feel a movie night coming up..." I say, with my most sophisticated smile.

"Sure. Why not?" He grins. "I enjoyed the last movie I watched with you."

I watch him put the CD into the player, dim the lights, and lower himself next to me. The heat coming from his big strong body is a turn on. I rub my hand up his thigh and across his package. He is deliciously hard beneath his jeans.

He does not turn his head to look at me, but there is a tightness to his jaw.

"You don't want me to?" I ask softly.

"Oh, I want you to," he growls, and he looks at me, cocking an eyebrow, like he's daring me to go ahead and better his performance.

"Good, because I am dying to."

In the blue light from the TV screen, he tilts his head back and closes his eyes. My heart is hammering dangerously fast in my chest as I knead him lightly with my fingers. His mouth opens and I hear the moan he lets out in response to my touch. It makes me feel powerful inside. This man really wants me. A voice in my head says something about Zelda, but I shut it up.

Slipping my hand under the waistband of his jeans, I pop his buttons open, and slide down the zip as I go, until I can wrap my fist around his girth. I bite my lip. Mmm… he is massive. I push down the desire to straddle his hips and ride him until we both come. My body is already hankering to have that big beautiful cock buried deep inside me, but not yet…I want to taste his cock.

I lean down, close my eyes, and quickly slide my mouth over his shaft. A few drops of pre-cum glistens at tip of his shaft and I lap them up hungrily. He tastes good, of clean skin, and him. I hear him gasp from above me so I quickly slide between his legs and look up at him as I pleasure him. I want to see in the changes in his breathing, his expression, and his eyes.

I slide my lips a few more inches lower so and he places his hand on the back on my head and guides me down slowly, tracing his fingers over the sensitive spot at the nape of my neck and making me squirm. Did he know how much this is turning me on? Probably. He seems to have a perfect read on my reactions.

I wrap my fingers around him, holding him tight, and begin to stroke him in time with the pace of my mouth. I move up and down, up and down, losing myself to this, forgetting everything but this.

I can hear his breathing getting labored above me as I move faster, working my tongue over every inch of him I can find, pausing and lingering at the top of his cock to swirl my tongue around him a few times. I can't look up and watch him. In the dark, it would be hard to see him anyway, but for the time being I'm more than happy to just focus in on his other physical reactions. The way his cock twitches in my mouth when I hit a certain sweet spot.

He lets out a growl and I know he is nearly at the point of climax. I stroke him with more intent, his cock lubed up generously by my mouth, and he thrusts back up to drive himself deeper into my mouth. His cock hits the back of my throat, but I can take it. I can take anything he gives me.

Anything at all…

Suddenly, I hear his breath above me seize, right at the moment the music from the movie swells and blots out the sucking sounds I'm making. His cock clenches in my mouth and he comes, running his fingers through my hair slowly and gently like he's asking me to take every part of him.

I don't need telling. I *want* to taste him.

I hold my mouth over him and swallow every drop of him, not wasting one little bit, satisfied with the knowledge that this time I'm the one in control, the one making him helplessly come. When I'm sure he's done, I sit back up and snuggle into my seat, watching him tuck himself away.

I playfully dab at the corners of my mouth, reminding him what we just got up to.

"Wow, that was hot," he murmurs, shooting me a devilish grin.

"So were you," I reply, and I turn my attention back to the movie.

Or at least, I pretend to until he starts undressing me.

Chapter Twenty-Three

LAUREN

I wake up groggy and confused, feeling like something isn't quite right. Then it comes to me all at once. I'm in Jackson's bed!

I turn my head and there he is, sleeping peacefully next to me, his breathing even. My heart melts. He looks, just…perfect.

I, on the other hand, feel like a mess. I just know there is mascara all around my eyes, a thought which is confirmed to me when I guiltily notice the smear of eyeshadow on his pillow. I carefully remove myself from the tangle of sheets and tiptoe out of his bedroom, collecting my various items of clothing as I do.

My purse is lying on the floor and I grope around inside to find my phone. It's 6:21am. Phew, still early. I stand there in his living room and dress quickly, looking around me at the evidence of last night. Empty glasses on the coffee table. The sofa all messed up with cushions on the floor. I pick them up and take the glasses to the kitchen sink.

I suddenly get a feeling that I shouldn't be here. I

need coffee and to take a shower desperately. I take a peek at Jackson and he's still fast asleep. Is it wrong to just leave? But it would be worse to stay. I breathe a sigh of relief as I pull the door of his house closed and it clicks shut almost silently. I don't know why I'm so glad to escape.

Danny is up and sitting on one of the bar stools in the kitchen, munching on granola. He eyes me with a smirk. "That's a convenient walk of shame."

Draco's at my feet, pawing for cuddles, excited to see me after my absence. "Very funny," I say, scooping him up and dropping kisses all over his adorable face.

"Give me details, woman."

"Ugh, I'm so thirsty," I say, balancing Draco while grabbing a glass, filling it from the tap, and downing it.

"Coffee?" he offers and starts pouring me a cup without waiting for my answer. He knows me. "So, are you going to tell me about last night? I gather it went pretty well? And you were so sure you were going to be tucked up in your own bed last night too..." He's got a cheeky grin plastered across his face.

I bury my face in Draco's fur. If he only knew what shy, prudish Lauren had gotten up to last night!

"Let's hear it," he prompts.

So I tell him about my wonderful date, but I don't tell him about how Jackson ate me out in the back-row of a movie theatre, or how he made me orgasm again and again like no other man before, or how we'd made love all night long, with only snatches of sleep in between.

Thinking back on it all, it feels like a dream. Unreal and amazing.

"And this morning?" he asks me, "I'm surprised to see you back so early! Or did Sexy and Mysterious have to go to work?"

"His name is Jackson! And—I kind of—left," I admit. "He was still sleeping."

"You didn't say goodbye?"

I chewed my bottom lip. "Yeah, I know. I just felt weird being there. It feels too soon to be waking up and having coffee together, like a couple, you know. I didn't know if he'd want me there or not. And I look a state!"

"You're a natural beauty, sweets," he tells me.

I know he is just being kind. No one looks good with Panda eyes except Pandas. "Besides," I tell him, "Part of me always feels bad. I'm deceiving him. He thinks he likes me, but it's only because of the potion. I wish he liked me for real."

"Please don't start going on about the potion again," Danny says, rolling his eyes. "It's probably just bullshit anyway, just like Andrea said."

I look at him, suspiciously. He's never taken Andrea's side ever, and he was the one who was trying to convince me to use it. "That's not what you were saying a few days ago."

"Well, I've had time to think about it more. I think you should just forget all about it. Love is a magical, magical thing. Who knows how it works! Just enjoy it."

"Do you know what he told me last night?" I tell Danny, still remembering snippets of the amazing evening. "He said he always went for blondes, but that he found me irresistible."

"Blondes are so overrated," Danny says, rolling his eyes even more dramatically this time, "I'm not surprised he's finally come to his senses."

"You're missing the point! It must have been the love potion that made him go for a brunette like me. It's proof that he is not fully in charge."

"I think you should forget about the love potion and just go with it, really!" he tells me, as he tidies up his breakfast things. "I have to go," he says, looking at his watch, "We've got so much to do at the project and I've got this silent retreat coming up so I won't be around for a few days."

I vaguely remember him mentioning a trip away. It seems so strange to me to pay to go somewhere and not be allowed to speak. But it's so Danny's kind of thing.

"Catch up tonight?" he offers me.

"Sure," I reply with a nod.

He envelopes me in a hug. "Ooooo… you smell of dirty, animal sex," he declares, pulling away from me, his eyes unnaturally wide and curious.

"Fuck off, Danny," I mutter.

"Putting dick before friends, now, are we?" he teases.

I shake my head at his antics as he's clutching his chest dramatically he flounces out of the room.

I can tell that's the end of the love potion discussion as far as he's concerned, but as I sip the steaming coffee something niggles. It should have been perfect, but it's not. I let the memories of last night flood over me. It had been amazing. And it wasn't just about the sex. Or the undeniable chemistry between us. We got along so well too. Surely, the way that we interacted couldn't have been contrived with the help of a spell. It seemed so real last night, but now I'm having doubts again.

My phone starts buzzing in my bag, but it's just my alarm. I sigh at the thought of work and Jackson.

"Hey Draco, did you miss me?"

He makes a sweet little sound and I rub his belly. Such a sweetheart. He looks at me adoringly with his big, brown, but these days slightly watery, eyes. Those eyes had been what made me fall in love with him all those years ago.

Peeking out from a little bundle of blond fur, scared and vulnerable. It had been love at first sight.

I pour his specially fortified, super-expensive dog biscuits into his bowl, then jump into the shower. Danny's has no idea how close to the truth he came when he said he smelled dirty animal sex. What Jackson and I got up to was feral stuff. I'm still sore between my legs and I have love bites all over my breasts. The hot water immediately makes me feel better, and I quickly pull on something presentable for work.

I can't help feeling guilty about just leaving Jackson like that so I pour him a cup of coffee and knock on his door on my way out to work. My stomach is in knots as always and I wonder if I'll ever be able to feel normal around him.

The door swings open and there he is, standing in his towel, just out of the shower and looking like a million dollars.

My eyes widen. His torso is glistening with wetness and all the things we did last night flash into my head.

"Ah, there you are. Want to call in sick?" he asks, one eyebrow raised.

I wish to God, I could call in sick, follow him inside, and take up where we left off. I have an incredible urge to run my tongue up his body, from his navel to his neck. "Yeah, I mean, no. I mean I want to, b-but I can't. I can't have them thinking I'm scared to show up at work. Anyway, I brought you this," I say, handing him the steaming mug of coffee. He takes it from me, his fingers brushing mine and making my heart beat faster.

"Thanks," he says, grinning boyishly, "You're a life saver. Listen, I have to go have dinner with my parents. Want to come along?"

"Uh…isn't it too soon?"

He frowns. "Is it too soon for you?"

"No," I reply immediately.

"Good. The only problem is it means I'll have to wait until dinner is over to get my hands on you again."

We smile at each other for a second. I *so* wish I could rip off his towel and go back to bed with him, but I'm going to be late if I don't get a move on. "I better get going," I tell him as I turn and walk away before I change my mind.

A hand closes around my wrist and I am suddenly yanked around and forward. I slam into his hard body. The masculine smell of his aftershave or shampoo fills my nostrils.

"Don't you know your place, woman."

"What?" I croak.

"Rule number one. Never leave the house without kissing your man."

"Oh, that." Yeah, I can live with that. I reach up on my tip-toes and kiss those sensuously full lips. He tastes of toothpaste, but even that is sexy. My heart starts racing.

He lets go of me and I nearly stumble and fall.

He catches me with a chuckle.

I step back on my own.

"See you later, gorgeous," he calls after me as I skip down the steps, my heart singing.

It's a beautiful crisp morning outside and I feel on top of the world. I'm actually looking forward to going into work too, I realize. I'm eager to show everyone that I'm not going to shrivel up and die because we have a good product and Mr. Montfort cannot see it.

That project is ours.

Chapter Twenty-Four

LAUREN

"Why would you want to meet his parents?" Andrea asks, raising one eyebrow. We are sitting at a café around the corner from where I work since Andrea had a meeting in one of the offices nearby so we decided to meet for coffee.

"I don't know, to get to know him better, I guess. Don't you think it's nice of him to ask me, though?"

"I think it's weird," she says, sipping her coffee and leaving a bright red lip-shaped stain on the cup as she places it back down again. "It's what? Your third date tonight? And he's already met your Mom and now you're meeting his folks?"

"I guess it must mean you're wrong and the love potion actually does work after all," I shoot back.

She gives me a look. "Oh, please. You're not still going on about that are you? It's complete and utter bullshit, seriously. I promise you."

"And now I'm going to meet his parents and they're going to be confused as to why he likes me so much because I'm not even blonde like his usual type and they're going to know something's up," I say. I know I'm being melodramatic, but I can't help wishing more and more that Danny had never interfered and put the stupid potion into Jackson's cupcake. It's constantly at the back of my mind and I can't secretly help feeling guilty about going to see Zelda in the first place. If I had never gone…"

"They're going to love you because you're a kind, intelligent, interesting woman. You're beautiful inside and out, Lauren. I wish you could see that."

"I wish I could too," I sniff. My stomach is in knots thinking about meeting Jackson's parents, even though I'm so flattered and excited at the same time.

"You could always come clean to him…" Andrea suggests.

I gape at her in horror. "He'll think I'm crazy!"

She laughs. "Exactly. It *is* crazy. So just forget about it and move on. Are you scared about falling for this guy? It seems to me like you're just making excuses to yourself."

I start to protest but shut my mouth. I'd never thought of that. Maybe she's right.

"I know you got hurt before, babe," she continues. "But you've got to let yourself move on and that means opening yourself up to the possibility of being hurt again. It's just the way it is."

"I can't believe I'm getting this advice from you," I scoff. "The girl who refuses to date!"

She looks away but I can see the tiniest sign of a smile. Is Andrea actually blushing?

"Have you met someone?" I ask her… Surely not!

"Maybe," she replies with a little smirk. She looks at her watch "Damn, I have to get back to work."

"But I want to hear more about this man of yours," I wail.

"Well you can't, as you've chosen your new boy over drinks with us tonight!" she scolds.

I know she's only joking. "You and Nina will be fine without me… and if we finish dinner early, maybe I'll bring him along?"

Her eyes light up, "Oh yes, please do!"

I look at her suspiciously. "Well, maybe. But only if you promise to behave. No embarrassing stories. And no calling me Lolly!"

She laughs as she agrees and we hug goodbye. I leave the coffee shop with my head in a muddle of angst about tonight, but I'm also curious about Andrea's mystery man who I can't wait to hear more about.

Back at the office, a huge bouquet of luscious yellow roses is waiting for me at my desk I can't stop the little squeal of joy that is torn from my throat. I rush forward and reach for the card. They can't really be from him, can they? It must be a mistake, surely. I never get sent flowers!

"They're beautiful," one of my colleagues, Jenny, gushes, full of envy, fingering the delicate petals.

I read the little card attached:

Can't wait to see you tonight, beautiful. Jackson

I can't help grinning. This guy seems too good to be true! I think of his gorgeous face and how much I want to kiss him again. Tonight, I think! He'd said he'd pop by and say hi after softball. But the unwelcome thought that it was all the effect of a gypsy spell puts a slight damper on it. I make a promise to myself that I'm going to have to do something about it.

At that moment, someone comes and stands behind me.

I turn around and my boss is rocking on his heels. Our eyes meet. He looks like he is about to cry.

I can feel my blood drain down to my feet. Oh, no. We haven't got the contract. I open my mouth and ask the dreaded question, "What is it?"

He shakes his head sadly, the way doctors in movies do when they have lost their patient.

For a second my shoulders slump. Danny and Jackson were both wrong. Mr. Montfort didn't just take offense to my shoe landing on his face. He took grave offense. He didn't give us the job. I swallow my disappointment. "I'm sorry, Mr. Jenkins, really sorry," I whisper. "Maybe I can go and see him. I'll apologize profusely. I'll show him that our system is miles better than anybody else's."

"Humph."

I stop talking and look at my boss in astonishment. He looks a bit red and a bit strange. "Mr. Jenkins?"

A massive grin breaks out on his face. Then he steps forward and clutches me by the forearms. "We got the deal!"

"What?"

He punches the air. "We got the Stanfort deal! And you'll be in charge of implementing it."

I can't believe my ears. Finally! I'm going to be doing something exciting. Out in the field. Not stuck in this depressing office.

I nod giddily as the rest of my team crowd around my boss. They're all laughing and happy. Barry, who called me stupid in the elevator after our presentation, claps me on the back and says he always knew I would carry the project home. Tom pops open a bottle of champagne. Sandy has glasses. Champagne flows. The other staff also gather around to congratulate us. A glass is pushed into my hands. Bubbles rush down my throat.

My life is almost perfect. There is only one thing wrong, but I plan to make it right.

I need to tell Jackson the truth.

Chapter Twenty-Five

JACKSON

They're already sitting at the table when I arrive, sipping on water and looking through the menu. Mom's looking great, she's done something new with her hair, I think. Dad looks tired but that's nothing new. I go around and kiss my mother's cheek. The familiar smell of her perfume fills my nostrils.

"How's work," Dad asks. Typical. Straight to the point and never one for chit chat. His brow is furrowed and his skin looks pale.

"Aren't you going to ask about how your son is before you start grilling him about work?" Mum scolds, tutting quietly.

I don't know how she puts up with him sometimes.

"I'm fine, thank you for asking, Mom," I say with a smile. "And work is coming along great, actually.

"I'll have the steak," Dad tells the waiter who has actually come for our drinks order.

"Darling, you know Dr. Goldstein told you no red meat," Mom says quietly.

"Oh, for goodness sake," Dad says huffily and slams

closed the menu. "I don't know *what* I'm allowed to eat, anymore. All these lists of forbidden foods and activities. What kind of a life is this?" He hands the menu to the bemused-looking waiter and crosses his arms over his chest.

"Would anybody like anything to drink?" he asks awkwardly.

I order a beer, Mom get a G&T for her and Dad.

The waiter goes off and Dad looks like he's been kicked in the balls by a donkey.

"Your hair looks nice, Mom, did you do something to it?" I ask.

She pats her hair and smiles softly. There are new shadows of worry under her kind eyes now. "Oh, you noticed. Yes, I got it cut. Your Dad thinks it's too short, but I love it."

"It looks great," I say, "Don't listen to him." I wink at her, trying desperately to lighten the mood.

Dad stands up and wanders off to the restrooms and I wait until he's out of earshot.

"Jeez, Mom, what is up with him? You guys just got back from your vacation a week ago, I thought he'd had a great time?"

"He did. We did," she says, nodding. "But you know what he's like. He thought relaxing in a spa resort for a week would solve everything and he'd be able to get back to work again. A few massages and saunas then everything would be fixed. But we went for a check-up yesterday and the doctor told him absolutely no." She glances around and whispers, "He even mentioned the R word."

My eyebrows rise. "The R word?"

"Retirement," she mutters.

"Really?" I lean back against my chair and can't imagine my dad not working.

"Personally, I don't think he should go back to work," she confides in me. "He just can't take the stress anymore. His heart can't. I want him to be around for as long as possible..."

"I'm sorry Mom, it must be so hard for you. I can see he's not great company at the moment. Who would have thought he had it in him to be even more difficult than he usually is! I thought he was going to bite your head off when you mentioned no red meat."

Dad gets back to the table. "Well, she's late," Dad says.

"Lauren's not late, Dad. We're early," I say, checking my watch.

Dad's reply is a grunt.

"I'm so looking forward to meeting her, Jackson," Mom says to me, smiling, always trying to keep the peace. "I can't believe you didn't tell us about her." She pats my hand affectionately. "Maybe you'll take her to David's wedding?"

"Maybe," I say, "But it's very early." I can't think of anything better than showing her off at the wedding. I'm sure she'd look absolutely stunning on my arm. But I'm not getting Mom all excited and start embarrassing me tonight.

Then I turn my head and see her.

She's walking towards our table, smiling in that gorgeous way of hers...and she looks stunning. In a tight sweater that shows off her delectable curves, fitted skirt, and black boots.

What I really want to do is drag her into one of the toilet cubicles and fuck her, but I stand and greet her with a chaste kiss her on the cheek.

"Hey, you," she whispers, her lip brushing my ear and encouraging me to carry on in my inappropriate line of thinking.

"Lauren, meet my parents. George and Judy."

"Hello, Mr. and Mrs. Miller. So lovely to meet you." Her voice is breathless and her smile is slightly vulnerable. I realize that she is nervous. She shakes my Dad's hand and gives Mom a peck on the cheek, then she takes the empty seat next to me.

I squeeze her hand under the table. It feels way too early to be doing this and I hope it's not going to put her off.

"So, Lauren, tell us about you! I love your necklace, how pretty. Is it from someone special? And what beautiful eyes you have. Are they green or hazel? I can't quite tell. So, Jackson tells us you're his next-door neighbor. How funny. My sister met her husband that way. Have you been there long?"

"Mom, calm down," I tell her. I don't want to scare away Lauren.

"It's ok," Lauren says, smiling at me and then back to Mom, "Thanks. And actually yes, this necklace is very special to me. It was my grandmother's. She gave it to me before she died. And I've been living at that address for about two years now."

I look at her delicate fingers, fiddling with the silver pendant in the shape of a rose.

"And what do you do for a living, Lauren?" Dad asks before Mom can say anything else.

"I work in a firm that specializes in sustainable business solutions. We help companies change their work flow, which not only increases their profits, but also helps the environment."

"That sounds like very important work," Mom chips in.

"What kind of education do you have?" Dad fires again.

Now, I'm remember why I never introduce women to my parents.

"Actually, I didn't finish school until two years ago. I had to study part time," she replies.

I'm proud of her for not letting him fluster her.

"My father was going through some financial difficulties so I had to start work in order to pay for my studies."

"An independent woman," Mom says, giving me a wink. "You'll have to watch out for this one Jackson."

"Where on earth is the waiter?" Dad says, changing the subject yet again.

Mom manages to catch someone's attention and soon a frightened-looking kid with a name badge that reads *Timothy* approaches us.

I immediately feel sorry for him. I bet it's his first day. As I expected Dad grills him about the menu and moans about Mom telling him he can't eat what he wants to.

"We'll both have the salmon," Mom tells waiter firmly, but she's smiling, as always, trying to keep the peace. Although I'm sure, Dad has never been this grouchy before. "Can you hold the butter, and we'll have green veg on the side instead of the buttered potatoes as well please."

The guy at the next table is having the steak with buttered potatoes and I swear he's smirking at me. Bastard. "Salmon and green veg sounds great to me," I say cheerfully. "Make it three."

"Make that four," Lauren says, and I could have kissed her right there and then.

Chapter Twenty-Six

LAUREN

"It was so nice to meet you both," I say, smiling, hoping desperately that I've made a good impression. Though, I can't say I'm very much taken with his father. The way he berated Jackson's poor Mom like that when she reminded him about his diet.

"And you, Lauren," his Mom says, smiling at me. She hugs me overenthusiastically and I'm glad my Mom isn't the only one who does that.

His dad gives me what I hope is a smile and shakes my hand firmly. For a moment, I see Jackson in him, the spitting image. Still holding my hand, he leans in towards me. We're out of earshot from anyone else. "I'm sorry if I seem like a bit of a grumpy old bastard, but I think you'll do nicely," he says. Then he grins. A real smile.

I feel myself blushing. He must have been just as gorgeous as Jackson in his day.

"I hope we meet again," he says.

I feel a strange flutter in my stomach. Maybe one day I'll be part of the family too… That's if Jackson doesn't run away screaming when he hears about the magic potion.

Jackson and his Mom come back from the restrooms and we say another quick goodbye before they finally walk off into the night and I breathe a sigh of relief.

I look at Jackson and giggle. "That was a bit intense."

"Yeah, sorry about my Dad. He really needs to learn to loosen up. I know he likes you though. I can tell."

"I hate to think what he would have been like if he *didn't* like me!" I say, grinning. I'm feeling almost dizzy with elation. Yikes, I got through the meeting of the parents. It didn't go terribly. His dad even liked me!

"What was my Mom saying to you?" he asks me. "When you came out of the restroom before dessert? You looked like a couple of naughty co-conspirators."

I can feel my face getting hot. I'm not going to tell him how she has 'such high hopes for us' and that, in her opinion, I'm the nicest girl he's dated for a long while. Nor the fact that she mentioned his great grandmother's diamond engagement ring! "Just that she was happy to meet me, that's all."

"Oh, I thought it might be about David's wedding. She's desperate for me to take someone. He's a close friend of the family. A little older than me, but we practically grew up together. Our families have been close for years."

I smile and don't know what to say. This is going to be really awkward if he doesn't ask me to go with him now.

"It's not for a while," he says. "But do you think you'd like to go with me?"

"I'd love to." I almost sigh with heavy relief.

He leans towards me. I know what's coming and my whole body melts into his delicious kiss. I can never get used to how soft his lips are, and the wonderful contrast between them and the shadow of slightly rough half-a-day-old, stubble, surrounding them. I drink in the very male wood-musk smell of his cologne and wish this moment could last forever.

He pulls away and we look at each other. I can't help the giggle that bubbles forth. I feel like a teenager.

"So, what do you want to do now?" He grins, playing with my fingers in his hands.

"My friends are drinking at a bar a few blocks from here," I say. "Or we could go somewhere else, if you'd prefer?"

"I'd love to meet your friends. Andrea and Nina, is it?"

I flush a little when I realize I must babble on about them a lot.

"You girls must be pretty close, huh?" he asks.

"We are. We've been inseparable since we were kids. There used to be a fourth member of the gang too, but she moved away a few years ago and we only meet her twice a year now."

"I've lost touch with a lot of my friends," he says. "They moved away or fell down the married-with-kids hole. I'm stuck with my buddy, Joe, and the crazy softball team that I usually need a couple of days to recover after a night out with."

"I bet Nina would get on well with them," I say giggling. "If there's beer pong involved, you won't get her away from it!"

We leave the restaurant and he gives me his jacket. It's freezing outside and I'm shivering in my oh-so-cute but not very warm dusky pink jacket. What a gentleman. I can't wait for the girls to meet him.

Chapter Twenty-Seven

LAUREN

"I know you're going to say I'm ridiculous but can you please just hear me out?" I plead with Andrea as we're eating dinner in one of her regular haunts: a trendy vegan place in Soma.

"Is it about that damn potion again?" she asks me, sighing.

"Well…"

"Look Laurie, you spent the whole week loved up with this guy, spending practically every moment together! I really think it's beyond that stupid potion by now. When are you going to realize he likes you because you're you!"

"I know, I know… But I just feel weird about it and I can't help feeling guilty. I just want to get some closure. For my own sanity more than anything else!"

"I thought you were going to own up to him? That's what you said the other night."

"I know…." I grimace. It had seemed easy after one too many cocktails and with Nina and Andrea both telling me how awesome he was when he'd gone to the restrooms.

But even though we'd spent most of the week together, I just hadn't had the guts to tell him.

"So, I'm assuming you have another plan?"

"I do… I was thinking about going to see Zelda again. I thought maybe she would have an antidote for the potion. Something to reverse the effects. What do you think?"

Andrea's shaking her head in disbelief, but to my surprise, she reluctantly agrees to drive me to see the old gypsy lady after dinner.

"Really?" I ask her, delighted. "You'll really come with me?"

"Sure," she says. "Why the hell not? Let's go see the crazy old woman again."

We speed off to the sketchy street in the Mission where Zelda lives and I find myself once again standing on her doorstep in the dark, knocking gingerly.

We're just about to give up when the door creaks open slowly and she appears, looking us both up and down with her cold beady eyes.

"It's me again, Lauren," I say as she doesn't seem to recognize me.

"I know who you are." She's frowning. "What do you want? I don't do refunds."

She looks like she's about to shut the door in our faces, but Andrea quickly pipes up, "I have cash," she says, waving a wad of money in front of the woman's face. "We want an antidote. For the love potion. We want to reverse it."

Zelda looks at Andrea, then me, then takes the money in her spindly hands, and counts it greedily. She looks up at me. "Reversing spells is a hundred more," she croaks.

"Jesus," Andrea starts.

"It's okay. It's okay. I've got it," I interrupt quickly. I pull out my wallet and hand over the money.

"Follow me," Zelda grunts.

"Thank you so much for bringing me here," I whisper to Andrea as we wander through her odd antique warehouse of a home.

"Wait here," she instructs, and scuttles off to the kitchen, returning quickly with another vial.

"Don't you need to read my tea leaves again?" I ask, and I see Andrea rolling her eyes. She was so cynical about everything! Which is why I still can't believe she just forked out four hundred dollars for me.

"Just give this to him, the same way as before. You have three days. After that it will be too late."

"Too late? But why? How does it work?" I ask her.

But she's already walking back through her lair. "Don't come here again," she tells us ominously, before shutting the door with a bang.

"What a charming old lady," Andrea snorts, shaking her head. "You'd think she'd be pleased she just made another five hundred bucks out of us!"

"I'll pay you back," I tell her, "I promise."

"It's a gift, Laur," she says, smiling. "Anything to stop you moaning that he doesn't really like you!"

I hug her tight. "You're too kind, but I'm going to pay you back, anyway. Don't forget, I'm rich now. I got a raise!" I say. Andrea earns a lot more money than either Nina or me with her trendy Google job, but neither of us liked to take advantage of her generosity.

"Whatever," she says. "I just hope this will be the end of it!"

"You still haven't told me about this guy of yours!" I tell her. "I can't believe you've actually fallen for someone!"

"Ugh, I never said that!" she exclaims, looking like

she's just eaten something disgusting. "Let's just say guys aren't usually the types of humans I enjoy hanging out with too. But this one's a bit different. He's great in bed, *and* he doesn't bore me to tears."

"Progress," I say and we both laugh.

She drives me back to mine and comes up to say hi to Danny. Despite his reservations about her, she has a lot of time for him. Well, she loves winding him up, anyway.

"Darling Danny, how on earth are you?" she says, grinning.

He pecks her on the cheek. "Always a pleasure," he replies.

He turns to me. "You're a sight for sore eyes, sweets! I feel like I might need to look for a new roomie soon."

"Aw, I'm sorry," I say, "I know I haven't been around much."

"I'm only joking." He grins widely. "I'm glad you love birds are getting on so well."

"And we have a solution for her ongoing issue," Andrea says, waving the little vial in front of him.

"What's that?" he asks, looking at me with raised eyebrows.

"I decided to buy the antidote," I say. "I just won't be able to ever relax until I know he likes me for me and not because of the potion."

He looks from me to Andrea and back to me again, confusion showing on his face. "And you agreed to this?" he asks her.

"Anything to stop the relentless moaning and self-flagel-lating," she replies.

Danny doesn't look me in the eye.

"Jeez, I haven't talked about it that much, have I?" I ask them. But the silence that follows answers my question for me and I wince. "Aw, sorry if I've been a bore about it."

"That's ok, sweets. How about we bake some peanut butter cookies this time?"

"Great idea!" I say. I'm so happy he's on board with it. Again!

"Ok crazies, I'm out of here," Andrea says. "Let's do Friday night girls only this week? Danny, that includes you if you're up for it."

"I'd love to but I won't be around," he says, mysteriously.

"Suit yourself," she says, shrugging, "But Lauren, no excuses for you!"

"I hereby promise to have a Jackson-free Friday night." As much as it pains me to not see him. Of course, things could all be different by then, once the rose-tinted glasses of the love potion have been removed. I desperately hope he'll still like me. It would be beyond depressing if he didn't.

"Night, Andrea, and thank you for going with me," I say as she walks out of the door.

"Didn't want to tell her about your silent retreat then?" I ask Danny with a grin.

"You know she wouldn't get it. And I couldn't be bothered to have a discussion about it. She's so cynical."

"I know… which is why I'm so surprised she was all up for getting the antidote to the potion!"

"Hmmm," he says. "Very odd."

"Maybe it's cause she's met someone," I suggest.

His eyes widen. "She's met someone? She's in love? Poor guy!"

"Oi! Andrea's a great catch," I say, frowning at him sternly. I'm feeling especially loyal to her right now. "But love? I wouldn't go that far. Small steps, eh?"

He laughs. "Right, sweets. I've got a busy day tomorrow. I'm off to slumber land. Are you actually sleeping here tonight then?

"Yeah, I thought we should have a bit of a break… I need to sleep!"

He grins. "Show off!"

"I haven't had any action for ages!" I protest. "Be happy for me!"

"You know I am," he says hugging me goodnight. "It's only cause I miss you! And poor Draco does too."

"Sorry Draco!" I say as I scoop him up and lie down on the sofa. It's so tempting to go and knock on Jackson's door. But I know he's working late tonight and tomorrow, but we have dinner plans for Wednesday. I'll figure out a way to get him to eat the cookie and then we'll take it from there…

Suddenly, I'm feeling incredibly nervous about the possibility of losing him forever but I know I have to do the right thing.

Chapter Twenty-Eight

LAUREN

"It's a disaster!" I whine. "Where could it have gone?"

Danny and I have turned the whole house upside-down looking for the tiny vial but it's nowhere to be found.

"Great," I say, slumping on the couch. "Now what am I going to do?"

I pick up my phone and call Zelda, but it just rings out. I try again and she answers. Her gruff voice startles me. Before I can say a word, she simply tells me not to phone her again and hangs up. I throw it to one side and sulk.

"Only one thing for it, now," I say to Danny.

"What's that then?"

"I'll have to come clean."

He frowns and says that he's not sure it's a good idea. I know all my friends think I'm crazy and I should just forget about the potion. But I want so much for Jackson to like me for real. A year down the line, I still don't want to be feeling guilty of hiding such a big secret from him.

"I can't hang around, sweets. Feather from the project

is picking me up any minute. We're driving up tonight ahead of the others."

"But I thought you weren't going till tomorrow. How come you're going early?"

"We're just going to stay in an Airbnb near Vacaville. It's not far from the retreat and it means we can check in early."

He looks all weird and I suddenly think I know why. "You've got a crush on this guy you're going with! You're sneaking up early together, aren't you!"

"Feather is a girl, not a guy," he says, looking away.

"Really? So how long has this been going on for? A girl? Seriously?" The last time Danny dated a girl was in about 2008!

He doesn't say anything.

"Why didn't you tell me?" I ask. "I think it's great you like someone. How long have you been seeing her for then?"

"Only a couple of weeks," he mumbles.

"A couple of weeks!? And you didn't tell me?" I feel a little betrayed.

He looks at me, his expression defensive. "Why didn't I tell you? Because you've been going on and on about this bloody love potion and Jackson, and *I* haven't been able to get a word in! I tried to tell you loads of times."

Thinking back, I know he's right. I've been a terrible friend! "Oh, my God babe, I'm so sorry! You're totally right. I've been so preoccupied with my own stupid problems."

"It's ok, sweets. I know. And they're not stupid. I understand. I've got something I need to tell you, actually. But I really, really have to go now!"

He blows me a kiss and hurries out of the door. I'm left shell-shocked. I can't believe he's been seeing someone, but all along, he's been making time for me, helping me bake and get ready for dates, listening to me moan, reassuring me. And now he has something to tell me! What if he wants me to move out? Oh, no!

"Draco!" I yell. I need cuddles, and immediately. I put the kettle on and go look for my lazy so and so.

"Draco, where are you, you smelly dog?"

I freeze. He's lying motionless on the floor next to my bed. I touch him and he whimpers. I breathe a sigh of relief.

"Oh Draco," I whisper. "What's up?"

He moves his head and looks at me. His poor old eyes wide and pained.

"Are you hurt you poor thing?"

I sink to the floor and cuddle him, stroking him gently with one hand, while scrolling down to the vet's number in my phone with the other.

Chapter Twenty-Nine

JACKSON

She's incomprehensible on the phone but it's something about Draco and she's hysterical. I tell her I'll be there right away. I leave the mess of paperwork on my desk and grab my jacket, texting as I wait for the elevator.

"Lauren!" I yell from the other side of her door after three knocks. "Are you ok?"

She eventually comes out, sobbing. Takes me by the hand and leads me to the sofa.

"What is it?" I ask her, my alarm growing.

"Draco," she sniffles.

"What's wrong with him?" I ask, hugging her tightly, fearing the worst, but honored that she's called me in her time of need.

"I took him to the vet…" she mutters through tears. "They said it didn't look good. He's got to stay there tonight. I don't want him to die."

She hugs me back tightly. Her back is trembling and she's crying desperately into my jacket. I just want to make it better, but I don't know how. It's a terrible feeling. I just carry on hugging her, knowing it's all I can do. "I really like you, Lauren," I suddenly blurt out. "I think I'm falling in love with you."

She draws in a deep breath, and ceases sobbing. Pulls back from me and looks up at me, those beautiful brown-green eyes blinking back tears. "Love?" she gasps.

"Yes, love. I think I have the worst case of insta-love this side of the Atlantic," I say teasingly, hoping to cheer her up.

But her eyes quickly fill with even more distress. "You don't love me, Jackson!" she suddenly cries out. "You just *think* you do! You're under a spell! It's the love potion. That's the only reason you think you love me. You'd never be with me otherwise. I'm not blonde, am I? You didn't notice me until poor Draco pooed on your welcome mat."

"What on earth are you talking about?" She's making no sense at all A love potion?

"I bought a love potion from a gypsy woman," she explains miserably.

I stare at her in surprise. "You bought a…love potion to use on me?"

She chews her bottom lip and nods.

"Right," I say slowly. "So when did I ingest this… potion then?"

"It's a long story, but I'll give you the gist of it. After I bought it I changed my mind, but Danny secretly put it into your cake. I didn't know he had done it and only found out when he rang me after I'd served it to you. I ran out to get it back, but you had already eaten it.

Ahh, the cake she'd given to me on our very first date. No wonder she had walked up to me as if I was a bomb that could have gone off any moment. I can't help but laugh when I remember her face.

She frowns. "Why are you laughing?"

"Oh, Lauren, my sweet Lauren, you don't understand. I have no idea what you're going on about with this love potion. All I know is that I didn't eat the cake."

Her jaw drops. "What do you mean, you didn't eat the cake?"

"I'm not really a cake person. And I ate a lot of your delicious meal."

"Oh," she says, her eyes softening and filling with wonder, "Really? You didn't eat it?"

I shake my head. "No, I didn't. So you can't blame the cake."

She frowns. "But you were already yawning and people only do that when they're losing interest, then after you ate the cake you changed. You were like a different person."

I laughed. "No, I wasn't. I pretended to yawn so I could ask you to get me coffee. Then you'd leave the room and I could disappear the cake."

"Why?"

"Because I hate red velvet cake. I hated it ever since I was child. We were eating in a restaurant and I got a fish bone stuck in my throat. I was choking to death. My mother grabbed somebody's dessert from the next table, which turned out to be a slice of red velvet cake. She smashed it and turned it into a ball in her hands. Then she stuffed it into my mouth, closed my jaw, and made me swallow it. It pushed the bone down and I could breathe again, but ever since that trauma I'm paranoid about bony fish, and hate the taste of red velvet cake."

"Oh," she whispers.

"I really liked you and I didn't want you to hurt your feelings that evening. You had gone to a lot of trouble to bake a different one just for me, and I was damned if I was going to make you feel bad. At the same time, I couldn't bring myself to eat red velvet. I couldn't believe it when your mother tried to offer me one. Hell, I nearly ran out of your house then."

"So, you really do have feelings for me then?" she asks in awe.

"I do, yes. I liked you from the first moment I saw you, bouncing up the steps, chatting away to Draco as if he was a person, not realizing I was just behind you."

"Oh, my God, that's so embarrassing."

"It was utterly adorable," I say, "I wanted to ask you out, but I thought you were with Danny so I told myself it was for the best. I didn't need the distraction what with the building work I had just taken on."

"Really?" she asks, wide-eyed.

I can hardly believe any girl this gorgeous could be so unsure of herself.

"When you first asked me to dinner I was smiling because I'd promised myself the next time I saw you, I would ask you out. But I chickened out and you got there first. I was very impressed."

"I was too, actually," she says and laughs.

Jeez, I really love this girl a lot. Maybe too much.

And then she's kissing me, her hands either side of my face. I kiss her back, with all my heart. Her lips tasting of salty tears and I kiss them all away.

She's laughing into my kiss and then crying again.

"But don't you think I'm crazy?" she asks. "I tried to put a spell on you!"

I can't help but laugh. "I think you're crazy, yes! But I love it."

She giggles through her tears but then she stops. "What happened to the cupcake, then? Where did it go?"

"I…" I stop suddenly. Oh, shit. She's not going to like this part.

"What is it?"

"Draco ate it," I confess with a grimace.

She stares at me in horror. "The whole thing? He's not supposed to eat stuff like that. He's old now, Jackson and he has a delicate system. I spend a substantial part of my income buying him the very best food and supplements." Suddenly she goes white. "Oh, my God! Dire consequences, she said. That's why he has suddenly fallen ill. Draco is never ill. Oh, no. He could die."

I go to hug her again but her body stiffens and she looks at me accusingly. "How could you do that?"

"Hey, hang on a minute. I didn't mean to hurt Draco. I actually held it out for Tyrion to eat, but Draco jumped up and literally snatched it from his jaws."

"If you had just been honest with me, I could have rushed him to the vet and told them to pump his stomach or something."

"I didn't know it wasn't anything but cake. My dog eats cake without any problems and the way he jumped up and stole it was like he was used to it."

"No, he did that because he never gets anything like that. I'm very strict with his diet."

"Anyway, all this happened more than a week ago so how can it be the reason he is ill now?" I argue.

"Who knows how long the medicine takes to show its effect."

"I'm so very sorry, Lauren. I know how much you love Draco and I would do anything to make it better for both of you."

She shakes her head sadly. "It's ok. There isn't anything you can do. I think I just want to be alone for a while. I need to think." A lone tear slides down her cheek making me feel awful.

I wipe away the tear away and kiss her on the forehead. "I'm sorry. I'm really sorry."

"I know. Can you please go now?"

I can see that she is blaming me because she needs someone to blame. "I don't want to leave you like this."

"I'm fine. I promise you. I'll call you later, okay?"

I stand up, feeling lost and helpless. It's a horrible feeling. "Text me if you need anything," I say as I walk to the door, but she doesn't reply.

Chapter Thirty

JACKSON

"Hey, Joe!" I say, trying to look happier than I feel.

"What's up, dude!" he yells, slapping me on the back. "I was early so I already ordered, hope that's ok?"

"Cheers, man. How's it going?" I ask, as I take a seat opposite him.

"Ah, you know. Can't complain."

"Things all better with you and Gina now?"

"Yeah, of course! I've been a good boy this week," he says, winking at me. "Need to save up bad boy credits for Tahoe, don't I? Can't wait! Gorgeous leggy blondes looking all cute with their snow gear on. They're gonna be lining up to strip off and get in our private hot tub!"

I remember then. Only two weeks until the big bachelor party. "I'm not going," I announce.

"What? All the plans are made. You can't not go. We've got three condos in Squaw Valley and last time I checked twelve of us going. We need to sort out a big grocery shop and then figure out some pranks for the groom to be." He's got a wicked grin plastered across his face and I feel sincerely sorry for the poor groom to be, David."

"I'm not going," I say again, this time even more firmly.

"Aw come on dude, it's gonna be epic! I've heard the chicks down there are crazy on spring break."

"How is that unlike spring break anywhere else?"

"You're only saying that because you're all loved up," he sniggers.

My expression must have given me away, because he practically pounces on me. "Whoa, what happened with the hot brunette?"

I shrug. I don't want to discuss Lauren with Joe or anyone else.

"Come on, man. Get if off your chest."

"I don't know. I thought it was going well. But she got crazy at me last night for feeding her dog some cake. Reckons I might have made him sick."

"Women!" he says, rolling his eyes. "They're so unpredictable. Gina gets mad at the weirdest things. Well, most of the time, I don't even know why she's mad. I just say sorry and buy her something."

I narrow my eyes. "Somehow, I feel like she has plenty of reasons to get mad at you!"

"Hey, whose side are you on?" he says, grinning, knowing full well what a handful he is.

"What you need to do is organize some grand romantic gesture," he continues. "Sweep her off her feet and make her feel like a princess. If she's worth the effort, of course."

The waiter places two steaming plate of buffalo wings in front of us.

"Best wings in the Bay area," he says as he takes a particularly plump one from the pile and pulls off all the meat into his mouth in one go, like a pro. "So good," he mumbles.

We chew in silence until he breaks it, "Or maybe you should just forget about this Lauren chick until after Tahoe?" he says, winking.

But Tahoe girls are far from my thoughts. Lauren's the only one I can think of. Inside, I'm hurting. Somehow, I have to win back her trust. I rack my brain to think what she would like. She doesn't seem like the kind of girl to lavish with flashy nights out and fancy hotels. She'd see through that bullshit. It has to be something really special.

"Daydreaming about Tahoe girls?" Joe asks me, grinning and as clueless as ever.

Chapter Thirty-One

LAUREN

"Any news, sweetie?" Mom asks gently, putting a cup of tea down on my bedside table.

I shake my head.

Since the vet is closer to my folks' place, I decided to wait here, in my old bedroom. I've been lying in bed remembering the good times with Draco. This was his first home. He was the cutest pup ever. The memory of his first night with me is crystal clear still. Mom and Dad had insisted that he learn his place and put him in a box filled with blankets in the kitchen, but he had cried so much I had sneaked down and brought him into my bed.

In the morning, Mom had found us in tucked up in bed together and she had pronounced that I had ruined the dog forever, but she was wrong. Draco did not become spoilt or unruly. I didn't have to toilet train him, he naturally knew to do it outside. With the exception of that time with Jackson's mat, of course, I've had no toilet problems. I glance at my phone but still no news from the vet. I wonder if poor Draco is still on the operating table.

"It's ok," I reply, sitting up and thanking her for

the tea.

"Well, I'm sure we'll hear soon and then we can go straight to pick him up."

"Thanks Mom," I say, "I just hope he'll be ok."

"Me too, darling. But he's a tough old dog, let's try and stay positive. Why don't you take another day off tomorrow as well? I'm sure Draco will want lots of attention after his op."

I smile weakly. I love my Mom for trying to be positive but the truth of the matter was that there was a high chance he wouldn't survive the surgery. It broke my heart to think of him lying there on the operating table.

"I need to go back in tomorrow. I told you about the big Montfort project, didn't I?"

She nods vaguely. Mom has no interest in work stuff. She doesn't even believe women should work. "Are you sure you're up for it, dear? I'm sure Mr. Jenkins will understand if you take a day off work. After all, your dog is sick."

"Actually Mom, he would. He would expect me to go in and I'll have to. I think I'll just stay here for a couple of days with you guys and go to work from here. At least you can watch over Draco.

"Of course, darling. Stay here as long as you want to."

The truth is I cringe at the thought of going back to my house. So empty without Danny or Draco. And worst of all, the thought of bumping into Jackson. He must think I'm unhinged after my crazy rant last night but I don't even care right now. All I can think about is Draco.

Mom pats me on the arm and tells me she'll be downstairs if I need her. I nod and manage to hold back the tears. But when she pulls closed the door they trickle down my face and I'm sobbing again. Why is my life such a mess all of a sudden? I've even messed things up with Jackson.

An hour drifts by as I lounge around watching old movies and not really concentrating at all. I call the vets for updates, but they can't tell me anything yet.

There's a knock at my door and my Mom pokes her head around. "Someone's here to see you."

"I don't want to see anyone," I huff.

But Nina is already at my bedside, hugging me. "This is so sad," she cries, "Draco's the best dog in the world."

"I know," I say, managing half a smile. "Thanks for coming to see me."

"I'll leave you two alone," Mom says, withdrawing.

That's fine with me because I'm ready to tell Nina what really happened. I blurt it all out to her.

She's sitting there with her hands over her mouth. "Oh, no! Do you really think the love potion made Draco sick?"

"I don't know..."

"What did the vet say?"

"He said Draco's arthritis has deteriorated massively over the last couple of weeks. It could just be old age, but we'll never know that for sure, will we? The gypsy did say there would be dire consequences if it went to the wrong person!"

"Draco isn't… a person though. Do you think it's the same for dogs?"

"I know it's wrong, but I just can't help being annoyed at Jackson for feeding him the cake. He has digestion problems too. Surely, he must have figured that out when he pooped on his doorstep!"

"But I'm the one who persuaded you to use the potion!" Nina gasps, "It's all my fault!"

"It's not! It's not," I tell her firmly. "It's Jackson's fault. He shouldn't have fed a whole cupcake to an old sick dog. What was he thinking?"

"Maybe he just didn't think…" Nina says, looking uncomfortable. "So, are you not going to see him again then?"

"I don't know." I sniff. I don't know what's wrong with me. I'm blaming Jackson although I know everything is my fault. I think guiltily about the bit of pizza Draco devoured too. "I've probably blown it with him anyway to be honest. What with my behavior last night." I hang my head in shame. I wish I could turn back the clock.

"But now you know that he does really like you," Nina says gently. "That's what you always wanted."

"Not like this," I say, starting to cry again. "He even said he was falling for me, but now I can't think of anything. I just want Draco to be ok."

"He told you that?" Nina's eyes are wide and she's got a goofy look on her face. "I really think you should at least give him another chance?"

There's a knock at the door and it's Mom. "I just phoned the vet again, love. They were just about to call you. Draco is out of surgery! And it went well. They are going to keep him in for a few hours to make sure, but we should be able to pick him up later this evening."

I can hardly believe my ears. "He's really ok?"

"That's wonderful!" Nina shrieks.

The three of us bundle into Mom's rusty old car and head straight there to pick him up.

"Oh, Draco!" I exclaim, when I see him. His big brown eyes light up and he whimpers affectionately as I gently embrace him. I'm crying again but they're tears off happiness and relief.

Mom drops us back at my place and Nina comes up

with me, carrying Draco as I open the door. He's still really groggy and we put him in his bed next to the couch.

"Jackson was meant to be coming over for dinner tonight," I say, glancing at my phone. "I really don't feel up to it."

"You've had a tough day, Lolly," she says. "I'm sure he'll understand if you change to another night. I'm glad you want to see him again…"

I smile. "I do want to see him," I tell her earnestly. "If he's still interested in me… God Nina, what have I done? I went crazy at him last night. He's probably having second thoughts."

"Have you heard from him today?"

I shake my head. "He texted goodnight last night. I never replied."

Nina is frowning. "When I said play it cool, this isn't exactly what I meant."

"I'll text him now…"

We spend the rest of the evening relaxing and watching over Draco. I start to feel a bit better. I try my best not to think of Jackson and what he is up to. I noticed his car wasn't parked outside when we arrived.

"I can't believe Danny's going on a silent retreat with someone he fancies! That would be soooo frustrating," Nina says, playing with her hair and laughing.

"I know. I guess they're just sitting there staring at each other?" I say and we giggle imagining it.

"Do you want me to keep you company tonight? I can stay over if you like?"

"That would be great, thanks." I smile at her and think how lucky I am to have such a lovely caring friend.

"Let's order pizza." She grins at me. "And have a movie night!"

Chapter Thirty-Two

LAUREN

"Wow, you're really good at this," Matthew Jones tells me, grinning. He's the main person I will be working with from Mr. Montfort's company.

He's got such an infectious grin that I can't help smiling back. "Aw, thanks! I supposed after my infamous presentation, you were probably expecting me to be really terrible."

He shook his head. "Actually no. I'd already heard a lot of good things about you."

"Really?" I can feel myself becoming warm with pleasure. "Do you think Mr. Montfort has forgiven me for the shoe incident?"

He laughs. "I can put in a good word if you like?"

"That would be amazing. Thank you."

He looks at his watch, goes to say something, then stops himself.

"Go on," I urge.

"I was just wondering if you wanted to go back to my

office and go through the survey documents with me. We can start analyzing the results this evening. It will save you time if we do it together. Then you can bring it all back here and work on it with your team. Only if you have time, though."

"Thank you. That would be great," I tell him, gratefully.

We pick up bagels and coffee on the way to his office. He takes me to their conference room where lots of files and sheets are spread out on the long table. We work together, munching on bagels as we go. It feels so exciting to be finally doing the project we've been working towards for such a long time, and it's five o'clock before I know it. A day at work has never flown by so fast.

"It's getting late," Matthew says, flexing his shoulder muscles. "You can go if you want. I can finish up from here."

I hesitate. I didn't really need to leave right now seeing as Nina was working from my house and looking after Draco for me. A job flexibility I really envied sometimes. "It's ok, I'd rather get as much done as possible. I don't have any plans tonight, so let's finish it. It'll be quicker with the two of us."

"I like your style," he says, flashing another glimpse of his white teeth, and handing me another file to look through.

We work steadily for another hour and a half. "Phew," I say, leaning back with satisfaction. "That's the last figure inputted."

He grins at me. "Well done. You were really fast. It would have taken me three times as long to finish on my own. Hey, you know you said you don't have any plans tonight. Let me take you for dinner to say thanks for your help today."

"Thanks, but I really should get home. I have a sick dog."

He shrugs. "That's a shame."

My phone rings. It's Nina. "That's my friend now with the latest update," I say, accepting the call.

"What's up, Nins?"

"Well, I'm just calling to say don't hurry back. I've just given Draco his medication and he's gone off to sleep."

"Right. Okay. I'll see you soon."

"I heard that. Your dog is fine and your friend doesn't want you to rush back. Are you hungry?"

I nod slowly. "Yeah, I'm starving!"

"Great." He flashes that smile again. "I know a place nearby."

We head towards the Marina to a cute little Italian place. We're walking down the street chatting when suddenly I stop in my tracks. Just up ahead of us Jackson is opening the passenger door of a car. His Mom steps out and kisses him. Oh, shit. My stomach lurches. He's so hot.

I don't know what to do. Did he see me? I drop my head quickly,

"It's just around the corner," Matthew says.

I follow him, even though what I every cell in my body wants me to do is run up to Jackson and tell him I've missed him like crazy.

"Do you know that guy?" Matthew asks, putting his hand on the small of my back and steering me towards the restaurant.

"Yeah," I tell him as we walk into the restaurant. "But it's a bit complicated."

We're seated at a little table with a checkered tablecloth and a candle in a wine bottle. It's very cozy. Some might even call it romantic.

"Ha. I bet you have lots of admirers following you around," Matthew says.

I can't help blushing. "I wouldn't go that far. But I'm sure you're pretty popular with the ladies yourself."

"Another life time ago." He gives a sad half-smile. "But it's a little difficult when you have a seven-year-old kid to look after. Not that I'm complaining. He's my best friend."

"You look too young to have kids."

"It wasn't planned, that's for sure. We tried to make it work but we ended up getting divorced about a year ago. I found out she was cheating on me."

"Oh, I'm sorry. That's awful."

"Yeah, I didn't take it very well. Actually, I was devastated," he admits, "But that was months ago now. The scars are healing. It took time, but I'm coming to realize I was never truly happy with her. It was one of those obsessive relationships, you know?"

The waiter approaches us with a bottle of red wine and pours out a generous amount into our glasses. He rattles off the specials for the day and we both order the same thing.

"I never thought I'd ever be able to trust anyone again," Matthew says once we're alone again, "But now I believe that no matter how much you've been hurt in the past, you just have to move on. Love again. Trust again. Hope again. So, was that your ex in the street?"

"Oh no, that's just someone I've been kind of seeing," I say. My stomach flutters when I think of Jackson. I want to see him so much.

"If it's any consolation I think he's absolutely crazy to be just *kind of* seeing you," he says, smiling at me, his blue eyes shining.

I feel that first sense of unease. Is he's flirting with me? I mean, he's gorgeous and charming... but I don't like dating guys I have to work with and more importantly, I can't stop thinking about Jackson. There is no man I want other than him. I decide that I need to be careful not to give the impression I'm a free agent. As soon as we finish our food, I lean back and put my napkin on the table. "I think I better go home. It's been a busy day for me."

"Of course," he says, smiling.

We're outside the restaurant when he leans in towards me. If I hadn't stepped back, he would have ended up kissing me. Now I know he's definitely flirting with me. Oh god, this is awkward. I take another step back as casually as I can and he immediately apologizes.

"No, *I'm* sorry," I say reassuringly. "I hope I didn't lead you on, or anything. I'm just not sure if this is a good idea. If we're going to be working together, you know?"

"No worries," he says with an oddly hurt grin. "You are way out of my league anyway."

My Uber pulls up and I waste no time in jumping in and waving goodbye. Phew!

Chapter Thirty-Three

JACKSON

I'm looking at the files on my desk but I can't concentrate.

Dammit.

I just can't get Lauren out of my head. I can't get the image of her walking down the street, smiling and chatting to that grinning, dumb surfer dude wannabe. And they'd gone into one of the most romantic little Italian places in the Marina! I feel so angry with her. Did she cancel dinner on Wednesday to see that loser too? I obviously got her completely wrong. She's just like the rest of them. Fickle, shallow, out for what she can get.

Screw her.

I need to clear my head. I walk down the street for a couple of blocks, breathing the crisp cold air deep into my lungs. I'll get her out of my head if it is the last thing I do. I grab a coffee at a place I've never been in before. It's all coconuts and kombucha, a hippy place. I sigh and agree to have almond milk as they don't do dairy.

"Hey, Jackson!" I hear and spin around. *It's Danny. Shit.*

"Glad to see you're switching to non-dairy," he says

cheerfully, "The dairy industry is atrocious. Worse than the meat industry even!"

I have no idea what he's talking about but I nod, and flash a smile. "Have you spoken to Lauren?" I ask him.

"Waiting for juice," he says, motioning to his phone plugged in behind the counter. "I was up at a silent retreat near Vacaville but after one night I was done! No electricity, no wifi, no talking!"

"Yeah, it was intense!" a chirpy voice chips in next to him and I turn to see the purple-haired girl it belongs to. She's got a ring through her nose and is wearing an outfit that makes me think of photos of my grandparents in the 60s when they went to Woodstock.

"Oh, this is Feather," Danny says, introducing us.

"I think you need to talk to Lauren," I tell him. "Draco got really sick. And she thinks it's my fault."

"What? Draco? Oh, my God, no!" he wails, and frantically makes for his phone.

I make my excuses and leave, wincing at the sour taste of my latte and swearing I'll never step foot in that place again.

Chapter Thirty-Four

LAUREN

Andrea has been texting me all day, apologizing for not being around in my time of need. Promising she'll make it up to me soon. And then my phone lights up again. Multiple messages from Danny flood in:

Sweets!! Oh my God I'm SO sorry. Poor Draco I can't believe it. I wish I'd known! I would have been back in a second.

Before I can reply to that, another message shows up:

Btw I bumped into Jackson. He told me. Are things ok with you two? He was acting a bit weird. I'm gonna give you the biggest hug tonight. Are you going out with the girls tonight? I'll come! Unless you don't feel up to going out. I'll cook you dinner if you prefer?

Aw, bless Danny. I'm relieved he's not still upset with me. And surprised that he's already back in town after the silent retreat. He wasn't due back until Sunday. But what did he mean by Jackson was acting weird?

I have still received nothing from Jackson even though I've sent him three messages over the last twenty-four hours. I start to text him again but then stop myself. I'll wait until tonight and get some advice from the others. As a matter of fact, I can't wait to see Danny again and grill him about what exactly transpired between him and Jackson.

～

"What do you mean he was acting weird?" I ask. Danny shrugs. He's looking super cute tonight with his beard all trimmed nicely and wearing a blue tweed flat cap. "He just seemed a bit aloof. Not that friendly."

"I don't think he likes me anymore," I say, my heart sinking. "It's funny how the love potion ended up having the opposite effect. Inadvertently."

"I can't believe you accused him of making Draco sick, though," he says, grimacing.

Draco's ears prick up at the mention of his name but he's soon dozing again, in his position snuggled between Danny and me on the sofa.

"I know… it makes me cringe now when I think about it," I say, stroking Draco softly. "He seemed fine about it at the time though. He forgave me for the love potion, said he was falling for me. But now nothing."

"Have you tried knocking on his door?"

I sigh. "I tried a couple of times, but he was out both times. I know he's working loads at the moment as well. He's trying to get his apartment refurb finished, and I saw him out with his parents last night."

"Didn't you speak to him?"

"I don't think he saw me. And anyway, I was with this guy from work. It would have been awkward."

"What guy from work?"

I tell him about Matthew and how our team will be working with him for a while and Danny gushes with excitement for me. But then I suddenly realize, I'm doing it again. "Enough about me! Tell me more about you and Feather! You didn't enjoy the silent retreat then?"

"It was not really the right circumstances, you know…"

I'm laughing. "That's what Nina and I were saying the other night! It must be the worst place to go with someone you like."

"It was," he says. "In fact…we were asked to leave."

"Really?" I gasp, starting to laugh. "Oh, wow! I guess they take the whole being silent thing pretty seriously then."

"I was I to know the walls were paper thin?"

I laugh. "Only you can go to silent retreat and keep everybody up all night listening to you screwing."

"They should be thankful for the free entertainment."

I giggle at the thought. "By the way what did you want to tell me before you left?"

"I got the funding to start my new business venture," he says, a note of pride in his voice.

"Wow! That's awesome! Congratulations, Danny! I'm so proud of you," I gush. I am happy for him, but I am also feeling more than a little relieved. Yay! Danny didn't want me to move out.

Danny preens.

"So you finally found someone to sponsor you, huh?"

"Yes, and you'll never guess who."

I stare at him blankly. I have no idea. The only person I can think of is Danny's estranged millionaire uncle but I know that's ridiculous. He's been hiding out in some Caribbean island ever since being investigated for tax fraud. I give up and shake my head.

"Andrea!" He grins. "Can you believe it? My old archenemy."

"Wow, that's amazing! I didn't realize she was that loaded."

"Apparently, so. She showed an interest in the project so I showed her my business plan and all my notes last weekend. She absolutely loved the idea and wanted to get involved."

It made sense. It was totally her thing. Yoga combined with charity, but the business side of things. Perfect for Andrea.

"I'm so glad you guys are finally getting on." I smile wistfully. I can't help remembering that I had missed all of this last weekend because I'd been with my sexy neighbor.

"I'm sorry things have gone a bit pear-shaped for you and Jackson." Danny squeezes my hand. "But I'm sure it's not too late. Why don't you try and talk to him in person?"

"I want to. It's just everything's been so crazy this week. What with Draco and work stuff going on."

"Don't be a chicken." He tuts at me. "I can tell how much you want to see him. It's written all over your face! And he lives a door away. So you can't even pretend that it's some big hardship to make contact."

"He thinks I'm crazy and he hasn't replied to any of my texts," I protest. "It's hardly a good sign, is it? Anyway, we're going to be late for the girls. We should head out. Is Feather coming?"

"She might join us later." He smiles, winking. "Bet you can't wait to meet her, huh?"

"You bet your bottom dollar."

We grab our jackets and run out of the door. I can't

help glancing hopefully at Jackson's door, but I know he's most probably not in anyway. But before I know it, Danny has run up to his door and bangs on it a couple of times.

"What are you doing?" I whisper fiercely.

"No harm in trying," he replies innocently, as he runs past me and jumps into his car. "See you at the bar."

I check my phone. It's just gone nine o'clock. There's no way he's in, I think to myself, but the door swings open. And there he is. Irresistibly gorgeous, as always.

"Hey!" I greet awkwardly. I'm totally not prepared for this.

"Hey, how are you?" he says but his eyes are distant.

"I'm really sorry about the other night," I tell him. "I know I acted like a lunatic and everything… I'm just crazy about Draco really. The thought of losing him got to me."

He softens slightly with hint of a smile. "It's ok. I understand, I'm just glad he's ok. Thanks for texting me and letting me know."

"Yeah…" I say and then I take a deep breath. "So, any reason why you never replied?"

He frowns. Looks down. "I'm sorry. I should have replied. If I'm honest, I've had a lot of my own stuff going on. With work, my parents, this weekend in Tahoe I have coming up with the guys."

"Go on…" I prompt. This doesn't sound like a man who is falling in love with someone. These sound like excuses. My heart is pounding and I'm scared. It feels so wrong that last weekend we spent so much time together and just five days later, I'm standing in his driveway having such a formal conversation with him.

"I'm just not sure if we're on the same page," he says, his jaw tight, a muscle ticking in his cheek. "I think I'm looking for something more serious than you are. I'm just not really into dating lots of people at the same time."

"Neither am I!" I shoot back instantly. "I'm not like that at all!"

He looks up at me again, studying my face.

I suddenly know exactly what he's talking about. "You *did* see me Thursday night!" I gasp.

"I'd have been blind not to," he says harshly.

"I'm sorry I didn't say hello."

"Yeah, it looked like you were on a date with another guy." There is a bitter expression on his face.

"No," I almost shout. "Not at all. He's a colleague from work," I explain in a jumble how about how he is from Mr. Montfort's company and how we had to work together that day. And we were both starving so we went for a quick meal.

He's standing there, taking it all in, looking at me earnestly with those gorgeous eyes. Then he takes a few steps towards me. "He's just a work colleague?"

I nod vigorously. "Cross my heart and hope to die."

He smiles. Finally. Dimples appearing. "I'm sorry I doubted you, but seeing you with that guy made my blood boil. I stopped thinking. I wanted to sprint over there and knock his teeth in. I've been like a bear with a sore head ever since."

"I'm sorry I didn't come and say hello. I wanted to. But I didn't know if it would be weird after how I acted the other night. And with your parents there too." I grimace, thinking about how awful it must have looked.

He takes my hand. "Want to come in for a…er…drink?"

"I'd love to come in for a…er…drink, but I'm meant to be meeting my friends," I say, distinctly remembering Andrea's demand for a girl's only night, but Danny did say Feather might be going along… "You wanna join?" I ask him, sheepishly.

"I thought you'd never ask." He lips curve upwards sexily. "But you're forgetting something."

"Huh?"

He tightens his hold on my hand tugs me towards him. I slam into his body and his mouth crushes my mine in a passionate kiss. Oh God, how I have missed this. I wrap my arms around his body and drink up his scent as I kiss him back deeply.

"Now we're ready," he says, as he pulls away, leaving me speechless and as ever, wanting more. His eyes are dark with desire. "But we better leave quickly or I'm going to have to throw you over my shoulder and carry you inside for that…er…drink."

"You throw me over your shoulder anytime you like," I say, "Apart from when I'm going out with my friends."

"I suppose I could stick to those rules," he says with a wink.

I giggle and grabbing his hand, pull him towards the steps. As much as I'd love him to drag me inside right now, I'm already so late. I figure Danny gave up waiting and went on ahead.

Hell, I feel intoxicated already. On life, on Jackson, on everything!

Chapter Thirty-Five

JACKSON

S o we're in an Uber, racing towards The Green Man and Lauren is giggling as she gets thrown into my arms when we turn a corner way too fast. I look at her happy face and it feels as if a sunburst has happened somewhere inside me.

"I got you totally wrong," I tell her, putting my arm around her and kissing her forehead, "When I saw you with that dumb grinning jock, I got so jealous."

"He does grin a lot," she teases.

"I'm serious. I thought you were one of those girls on Tinder. On a different date with a different guy every night."

She laughs. "Oh, my God! I'm not like that at all. In fact, I might be an incurable introvert."

"I'm glad to hear that. I want you all to myself."

"That's fine with me," she says, smiling.

She looks so happy I make up my mind to do everything I can to keep her that way.

We turn another corner with such speed that we slide

towards the other side of the car. "Take it easy, man!" I yell to the driver.

He grunts and slows down a little.

"The slower the better," I whisper, kissing her lightly on her beautiful mouth. "I want you to myself for as long as possible. You look beautiful tonight, by the way."

"Thanks," she mumbles, blushing and looking away.

I love that she can't take a compliment. She truly does look amazing, though. Her long wavy hair is tied in a high ponytail, her eyes dark and seductive. I want her more than she could ever know.

Chapter Thirty-Six

LAUREN

I walk back from the Ladies slowly, relishing the scene before me. My best friends, my darling roommate, and my new beau. All getting on like a house on fire!

Andrea glances round, spots me, and waves me over impatiently. She's looking particularly striking tonight with her normally dead straight bob fashioned into sexy waves, with a pink silk scarf tied around her neck.

"What is it?" I ask.

"I've got a surprise for you two!" she says, grinning at Nina and me. "Close your eyes!"

I look at Jackson and he shrugs. There is indulgence and amusement in his eyes. It makes me feel secure and I feel a flutter in my tummy as I turn to look at Danny, but he doesn't seem to know what's going on either.

"Ok…" I close my eyes and wait, feeling like a complete idiot.

"Guess who it is!!" a screechy voice yells out.

I instantly know exactly who it is.

"Pam!" Nina and I both cry out in unison. There are

animated hugs all round. Oh, my God, this day is turning out to be perfect.

"It's been years!" Nina says, "We thought you'd disappeared off the face of the earth!"

"Years? What the F are you talking about? You see me twice a year and I always send you all the best cat videos!" She grins, sticking her tongue out. Her hair is shorter than before, cut into a cute auburn bob, and she's lost weight too.

"You look great, Pam," I beam. It's so good to see her.

"So is this the fourth member of the gang?" Jackson says, smiling. "I heard you'd gone AWOL."

Everyone turns to look at me.

"I didn't say *that*!" I protest. "Just that you'd moved away and we never see you hardly anymore."

"Aw, I miss you guys." Pam smiles, and then shakes Jackson's hand. "I'm Pam by the way. And you're obviously the sexy neighbor."

To my surprise, I see Jackson's cheeks darken. Wow, he too, can be embarrassed.

"Good to meet you. So, what brings you back to town?"

"Well…" she says, looking all pleased as punch. "I've got something to tell you all."

We're all looking at her expectantly, waiting for her news.

"I'm getting married!" she yells, throwing her arms up and shaking them madly.

A cacophony of 'Wows and 'Congratulations' and hugs follow the announcement then all the questions start.

I, for one, am dying to know more about this mystery fiancée of hers. "You kept that one quiet, sneaky," I scold.

"It's been a bit of a whirlwind, actually," she gushes. "He totally took me by surprise. Swept me off my feet."

"How romantic," Nina squeals, holding her hands to her mouth.

"So, you met him in Africa while you've been working for this humanitarian project?" Andrea asks, as Jackson disappears off to the bar to order another round of drinks.

"Yeah, I guess I did the cliché thing. He was my boss." She giggles. "I thought he didn't like me to start with, but obviously, he did… To be honest, I can't believe he asked me to marry him. I thought it was just a fling. You know, the heat gets into your blood and makes you do crazy things, but marriage? Whoa!"

"You didn't use a love potion, did you?" Jackson asks on his return.

Everyone bursts out laughing except me.

"A love potion?" Pam echoes, looking at us all with a questioning look.

"It's a long story. I'll tell you all about it later," I mutter, my cheeks burning. I guess I should just be glad Jackson could laugh about it now.

"Aww, I've missed so much being with you guys. I can't wait to hear all the gossip."

I look around to see where Danny's got to and see him canoodling with a purple-haired girl at the bar. "That must be Feather," I whisper, raising my eyes in the direction of the bar.

"Yep, that's her," Jackson confirms.

Danny sees us staring at him and sheepishly takes Feather's hand.

"Come and introduce us!" Andrea yells.

Then he comes over alone.

"Everything ok?" I ask.

He looks down. "Feather's got something to tell you, apparently," he says to me, shrugging his shoulders. "Do you mind talking to her alone?"

I've no idea what she's going to say but I wander over to talk to her. She's petite and pretty but in a very tomboyish way and I can see why Danny likes her.

"Hey, Feather, it's so good to meet you!" I say, kissing her on the cheek. "Danny said you have something to tell me?"

When she relays her story, I'm speechless for a minute. Then I burst out laughing.

"I'm so glad you're not mad at me!" she says.

I shake my head, grinning. "Can we tell the others?" I beg her.

She shrugs. "Sure, why not. They're gonna think I'm a loon though."

"They're gonna love you!" I reassure her. I just know she's going to fit in fine.

We join the group and Danny introduces Feather to the girls.

I take a deep breath. "So, Pam... Do you want to hear the love potion saga?" I ask her.

She nods eagerly.

We tell it together, right from the beginning, Nina starting with the story about her colleague from work. Andrea piping up about how she thought it was bullshit from the get go. Me and my horror as I realized it was too late and then returning to Zelda for the antidote which mysteriously disappeared.

"You didn't tell me you bought an antidote," Jackson says with a laugh.

I grimace. "Andrea bought it, actually."

"So, what happened?" Pam asks, her eyes wide, "Did it work? When did you tell him?"

I shake my head. This was the part of the story that made me the most embarrassed—my outburst when I was upset about Draco.

Jackson then comes to my rescue and tells a mostly flattering version of the turn of events, "And then she goes crazy at me because I *didn't* eat the cake! And blames me for poor Draco getting sick."

"Aw I'm sorry," I say, as I laugh.

He gives me a kiss on the forehead to show all is forgiven. "How can I be mad at you for wanting me to love you?" he asks.

I can see Nina practically swooning behind him. I turn to Andrea and I'm surprised she's not making a nasty face,

"All's well that ends well," she says with a little laugh. "But hopefully, we've all learned our lesson about contacting strange old gypsy ladies in the Mission from now on."

She looks pointedly at Nina and me, and we roll our eyes at her.

"That's not quite the end to the story…" Feather says, smiling but shaking her head in shame at the same time. "You see when Danny and I started seeing each other, I was feeling kind of insecure. It's silly, I know, but he told me he usually dates guys and I was worried he was going to get bored, or I wouldn't be enough for him, or something stupid like that."

"You didn't waste money on that woman too, did you?" Andrea asks, horrified.

Feather crinkles her face. "Worse."

Now she has everyone's full attention.

"Danny told me all about the cupcakes Lauren made," she explains. "So, when he invited me upstairs for a quick coffee that Sunday morning before sunrise yoga…"

Danny's eyes are wide as he stares at her.

Now I realize this is the first time he is hearing the story too.

"You told me to put some in a box to take with us," she

says looking at him. "And when I saw the special one with the pink wrapper that he told me had the love potion in it, I just couldn't help myself. I swapped the case with a regular one. And took the one with the love potion."

"You did what?" yells Danny, and then realizes the implication. "Hang on a minute, did *I* eat the potion?"

"No!" she says, quickly. "Don't you remember, I was asking questions about it in the car? And then you said something about dire consequences and I didn't want to take the risk."

"So, what did you do?" asks Nina.

She shrugs. "I threw it out of the car window when Danny wasn't looking."

We all burst out with laughter.

"I'm glad I'm not the only crazy one around here," I say, feeling less embarrassed about how stupid I've been. It would have made my life a lot easier if I'd known about this a bit earlier though, but with Jackson standing by my side, his arm around me, my friends all happy and reunited with Pam, I couldn't care less. Things couldn't be better!

"Now it's my turn to confess," Danny pipes in.

We all look at him in surprise.

He focuses his attention on me. "You know how we couldn't find the antidote?"

I nod. "Yeah?"

"Well, I threw it away."

My jaw drops. "Why?"

"Because I didn't care if it was the love potion that had made Jackson fall for you. I knew he was a good guy, and I'd never seen you so happy."

"Oh Danny," I whisper as I hug him. He really is a true friend. I couldn't have asked for a better roomie.

Our hug is cut short when Jackson pulls me to him. "That's enough now," he growls.

Everyone starts laughing again.

"So, ladies," Pam yells, gathering us together and handing out tequila shots. "I've got something I need to ask you."

We chug down our shots, grimacing, then laughing.

"Go on then," I urge. "What is it? We're not all moving to Africa, if that's what you're asking."

"Although I would love to come and visit," Andrea adds.

"You should all come and visit. It's amazing out there. But no, that's not it... Would the three of you do me the huge honor of agreeing to be my bridesmaids?"

Chapter Thirty-Seven

LAUREN

J ackson closes the door and leans against it. Tyrion dashes madly around him. He leans down and gives the dog a good rub on his head. Satisfied, the hound moves away and goes to lie on his bed. He straightens and looks at me.

"Now it's my turn," I say with a wicked, wicked smile.

There is no answering smile. "Do you realize you messed with my head tonight?"

I widen my eyes innocently. "I did?"

"Didn't anyone ever teach you, telling a man you're not wearing panties while he's out with you drives him crazy?"

I try not to smile. "Someone called Andrea might have mentioned it to me."

"Hmm…Did Andrea also tell you what happens to such…cock teasers?"

"She might have."

"Good. So what happens to you next might not be such a surprise."

His eyes never break contact with mine, as I start

backing away. "Well, you can't really blame me. You're so hot, I can't help myself."

He chuckles and takes a step forward. "You'll need to come up with a better excuse than that."

I take another step away from him. "What are you going to do?"

"I'm going to satisfy the ache in my cock."

There is something very different about him tonight. I take another couple of steps and come up against the dining table. He closes the distance between us. His hand goes up my skirt and between my legs. "You're fucking soaked," he purrs. "Why are you so wet, Appleton?"

"I don't know," I lie. God, I don't think I've ever been this horny. My need for him is like a throb between my legs.

"I think you do," he drawls. "I think you are looking forward to your punishment."

I lick my lips. "I don't like the look in your eyes."

"I don't like that you haven't opened your legs for me, yet."

I start to squirm against his hand. I want more. I want his fingers inside me. Then his thick hard cock. His hand moves away. Suddenly they are in front of my chest. Before I know it, he has ripped my blouse open. Roughly, he pulls it off me and discards it.

Excitement rushes through my veins. His hands move around the back of me to unclasp my bra. It falls to his feet. He looks down at my nude breasts, his eyes possessive, primitive. As if I am something he owns. It makes my belly tighten. He makes short work of my skirt and flings it behind me. I stand pressed up against his dining table buck naked.

My breaths comes fast and shallow and my nipples are erect. From the cold or arousal, it's hard to tell. Not that it matters. His eyes watch the way my breasts rise and fall. Instinctively, my hands come up to my chest to cover it, but he catches them and pins them behind me.

Then his other hand moves to my folds. He rubs them around and I can't help the moan that escapes my lips. He looks at my body twisting, my breasts pushed forward and there is an expression of primitive triumph in his face.

"You're mine," he mutters harshly. "Tell me you're mine."

"I'm yours," I say immediately. My voice sounds shaky.

His head moves as he catches a nipple in his mouth and begins to suck. Hard. Harder than he has ever done.

I gasp at the strange sensation. "Oh," I cry as he bites down gently.

He takes the other one in his mouth and does the same.

I squirm and writhe helplessly.

Suddenly, he takes my shoulders and spins me to face the dining table. "Bend," he commands, pushing me down firmly.

The table surface feels cold and makes me jump. His hands move to my wrists and pushes them so they are flat on the table, up above my head. He leans over me, and pushes me further up, until my hands are over the far edge of the table. He's molding them down.

"Don't move," he orders, his mouth close to my ear, his breath hot and urgent.

He straightens and suddenly yanks my hips back, so I am stretched out tautly across the table and my feet leave the floor and I have to hold on to the table edge. The position makes me tremble a little. I exhale in shock as he gently kicks my feet wide apart.

With my ass in the air and my legs wide open, I feel totally exposed to him.

There is a long moment when nothing happens. I dare not turn around, but I can feel his eyes on my body. I try to imagine my white skin against the dark table. Like a sacrifice. I jump when I feel his hands on my hips again, sliding slowly down over my heated skin, his thumb tracing my spine, following the little bones down to my tailbone. I gasp when it moves down to the fully exposed crack of my ass.

A long finger pushes into my wetness. That finger dips in and out. "Just checking how wet and ready you are for me," he says.

I arch with pleasure. Everything is so gentle and so smooth it is a shock when he suddenly leans over me again, his hard weight pushing down on my back. I can feel every inch of him pressing down on me. His powerful hands cover mine, and his breath is hot in my ear. His tone is soft, a challenge. "You want me to stop, Lauren?"

"No," I cry hoarsely. The surge of desire in my body for him to totally dominate me and take me in any way he wants makes me feel almost drunk with need.

He straightens and I hear the rustle of his pants being opened, the sound of the condom. Then he grasps my hips as if he can't get enough of me and impales me, forcefully and inexorably, stretching and filling me, until it seems as if his thick cock reaches the very depths of my belly. A place no man has gone before. The tightness makes every tiny moment feel incredible.

"You're so fucking tight," he growls.

I can't think of anything cute or flirty of sophisticate to say. All I can do rock my hips back and forth. He grasps me around the waist so I can no longer move. He wants to take that control back. I become still. He starts to thrust into me, shallow quick movements that make my rub against the table.

I cry out with pleasure.

Suddenly, he begins to fuck me deeper and deeper, burying himself up to the hilt inside me. My pussy gets wetter and wetter. I can feel my juices dripping down my thighs. My moans turn into a groan as I find my release. He carries on slamming deep into me as I totally lose it and scream. Suddenly, I feel him join me over the edge. For a long moment he doesn't move, allowing us both to come back down to earth. Slowly, my eyes focus again and my breath becomes less ragged. I turn my head and look at him. His hair has fallen over his forehead and he looks like some sort of avenging angel.

His mouth meets mine. Incredibly, our kiss turns him on again and I feel him harden inside me. He straightens and pulls out of me.

"Don't move," he says. Getting down on his knees, he licks my pussy clean. Then he scoops me in his arms and takes me to his bed, where he has me all over again.

Chapter Thirty-Eight

LAUREN

I'm early to meet Andrea and as I walk towards the restaurant, I spot her getting out of a flashy Mercedes. She stops to kiss the well-dressed gentleman in the driver's seat before striding towards me, her long chic coat billowing behind her.

She sees me and smirks. "Ha. Caught you, looking."

"So, who was that then?" I inquire. "I see it pays off to turn up ten minutes early to see who drops you off!"

She's still smirking as she slips her arm through mine and we stride towards the restaurant. "Well, I had an amazing afternoon of great sex! What did you do?" she says, throwing back her head and laughing.

"Same!" I giggle.

"We're like Cheshire cats," she says, pulling open the door with gusto and waving her hand for me to enter.

"Like the cats that got the cream," I agree, smiling, as I walk past her. And then my hands shoot to my mouth in horror as I realize the unintended innuendo in my remark.

Andrea throws back her head and shrieks, unable to control her laughter.

People sitting at tables around us are staring and I just know I've turned a crimson red."

"Classic, Lauren." She shakes her head while draping her arm around my neck.

We select a table in the corner next to the window.

"I love to see the life of San Francisco, played out in front of me," she mulls as I take my time to consider the menu, "And not being able to hear any of it is the best part."

I look up to see what's going on and we witness some kind of disagreement between a cyclist and a pedestrian.

"I'd like to be able to hear what's going on at the moment," I say, watching the man with the bike throw a final insult with the wave of his arm before jumping back on his cycle and riding away angrily.

"Oh, it's far more interesting to make it up," Andrea suggests with a wicked look in her eye. "I bet briefcase man had a sordid affair with bicycle man's mistress."

"Oh," I say, sarcastically. "Not even the wife. The mistress! What a twist." I roll my eyes. Andrea knows how I hate infidelity. "So, who were you fucking all afternoon then?" I ask her, arching my eyebrows. "Is he the guy you were talking about the other day? The one you might actually have an ounce of feelings for?"

"Maybe," she says slowly. "

A waiter appears. "Can I take your drinks order ladies?"

We decide on a bottle of wine, because, it's Saturday after all, and there's no sunrise yoga class tomorrow. I've already promised to go to the next one. As well as, of course, the fact that we haven't had a proper catch up just the two of us in such a long while. And, oh, just so many reasons for wine.

"How's it going with this guy then?" I ask.

"Ricardo is extremely intellectual. And a health freak. And half-Italian," she says, her mouth widening to a sly smile.

"Very nice," I agree. "Do I want to know how old?"

"A mere 45," she replies.

"A spring chicken," I murmur.

"Don't diss older men." She sits up and wagging her finger knowingly. "They *know* what they're doing in bed. And if they can't get it up, they go down on you for hours. It's a win-win situation."

I can't help but giggle. "Well, I'm glad you've found someone only twenty years your senior. Do you think it might be serious?"

"Serious, pah!" She makes a face. "We are very much on our own terms. But let's just say if things continue as they are, he *might* get an invitation to our Friday night soiree one week."

"Wow, that's commitment," I say, and we laugh.

"Enough about him, anyway. If I talk too much about him I'll just get bored and ruin it. How's your dashing Jackson?"

"I think I could happily talk about *him* forever and never get bored," I gush.

"Ugh, please don't. That would bore me." Andrea grimaces. "I bet you guys have nicknames for each other already," she says shaking her head.

I nod happily.

"Oh my god, you guys are too cute. So, what's your nickname?"

"You'll laugh."

"Probably, but you're not leaving this restaurant until you tell me," she warns.

"All right. It started off as Appleton pie and now it's little pie."

First, her eyes widen, then she bursts out laughing. She laughs so hard, she starts cackling like a hyena.

The best part is I don't feel silly or care. I love our names for each other. My heart flutters when I think of him.

She wipes her eyes with the napkin. "And where's lover boy now? Did you wear him out this afternoon?"

"He's having dinner with his parents," I say primly. "We're meeting up later."

"Didn't you want to do another dinner with the in-laws, then?"

"He invited me but I said I was hanging out with you."

"Shucks. I'm honored."

The waiter pours our drinks and we ask for another few mins before we order.

My phone pings and I see Jackson's name pop up.

"Are they already done with dinner?" she asks.

I nod, smiling as I read the text that tells me he misses me. "Yep, seems like it."

"Old people eat so early," she says. "We'd better order then, so you can rush back to Jack Sausage."

"Ha, ha, very funny." I wave the waiter over. "I'm starving."

"Me too!" She nods. "I guess we both built up a bit of an appetite this afternoon."

Chapter Thirty-Nine

LAUREN

He's kissing me before I'm even inside his house. His arms pulling me in closer, mine wrap around him, feeling the warmth emanating through his T-shirt. I relish the feel of my hands running all over his beautiful sculpted body.

"Hey," he whispers in my ear between kisses on my neck. "I missed you. I've been thinking about you the whole time."

"Me too," I whisper back, my heart already racing.

He takes my hands and leads me inside where he's transformed his living room.

"Oh!" I gasp.

The sofa is now pulled right in front of the huge TV. The coffee table has been cleared of the usual books and in their place sits a bottle of champagne on ice, a bowl of chocolate-dipped strawberries, and two champagne flutes. The sofa has been adorned with plenty of cushions and a huge fleece blanket.

I turn to him. "You just did all this?"

"Do you like it?"

"It's perfect! So, what are we watching? Please don't say a horror movie!"

"You love horror movies!" he teases, laughing and then adds, "You'll see. Take a seat. Champagne?"

I take off my jacket and boots in about two seconds flat then jump onto the sofa, accepting the glass of champagne with a giggle.

He dims the lights and joins me. He's pointing the remote at the TV and pressing a few buttons until the opening credits of the movie start rolling. He's picked the Shining. I shake my head.

"Plenty of scenes for you to hold on to my biceps," he says with a wolfish look.

"You know I can't decide if you're a bad boy, or the most romantic man I've ever come across," I tell him, raising my eyebrows. "I guess you must be a bad boy."

He pulls a moody face with a scowl, runs his hand through his hair and leans towards me, arching an eyebrow.

I burst out laughing and his face drops.

"I guess I need to work on my bad boy look a little more…"

"I like you just the way you are," I whisper, reaching for a chocolate strawberry and holding it in front of his mouth. He licks the chocolate slowly, making sure his warm velvet tongue licks my fingers too. Watching him makes me remember licking him and my mouth begins to water.

He returns the favor and I deliberately suck the strawberry in the most provocative way possible.

Jackson pulls me in closer, kissing my cheek, my ear, my neck.

I turn to face him, kissing his beautiful lips, letting my tongue explore, finding his, feeling his hand on my breasts.

Chapter Forty

LAUREN

We wake up late after a glorious night. I turn to him and grin, no longer caring what my mascara is doing.

He rolls on top of me and kisses me, stroking my face affectionately. I want more but he pulls away, wanders off.

I sigh with utter happiness and lean back against the pillow, watching the silhouette of his gorgeous naked body move around in the dimness of his bedroom.

"Are we ready for light?" he asks as he places my coffee on the table next to the bed.

"Sure," I say, yawning and stretching, basking in the warm rays of sunshine that flood over my body as he opens the blinds.

My phone pings, but I don't even glance at it. I'm not planning to answer whoever it is, anyway. Not at least for a couple of hours.

"Matthew Jones?" Jackson asks, seeing the name on the screen. "Isn't that the guy from your work?"

"Yeah," I say, sipping my coffee.

"What's he doing texting you on a Sunday morning? Isn't that's a bit weird."

"Oh, he's probably just giving me some info for next week. I told you I'm going to be working for him for a while."

"You didn't tell me that," he says frowning, "I thought you finished everything that night."

"Yeah, exactly. We finished putting it all together now my team and I will be working on it and liaising with him. He's the guy on the other end, you know?"

He frowns again. "He must have feelings for you."

"He barely knows me. And he's short-staffed. It just made sense, there's nothing more to it." I look at him and smile slyly. "Are you a little bit jealous?" I poke him affectionately in the side.

"Of that little surfer kid? Ha. Not a chance."

But I can tell otherwise and something inside me loves the fact that my beautiful Jack Sausage is feeling a little possessive over me.

I put down my coffee and lie on top of him on the bed. We're completely naked. The feeling of his skin next to mine is just wonderful.

"Look," I tell him, gazing deep into his gorgeous green eyes. "He did get a bit flirty when we went out for dinner that night, but I put him straight immediately. He's friend-zoned. I promise."

His face softens and those gorgeous dimples appear again. "Maybe I'll have to put him straight myself, just to make sure."

I giggle. "What are you going to do, challenge him to a duel or something?" I know it's silly but the idea of two gorgeous men fighting over me gives me a bit of a kick.

He rolls his eyes. "I'm serious. I don't want him getting any ideas."

"It's fine. He won't." Then I lace my fingers in his hair, and softly steering his head towards me, I kiss him until he kisses me back and wraps his arms around me.

He brushes his lips down my neck, barely touching the skin. His lips feel softer, more luxurious than ever. I roll my hips, drawing him up and down my wet cleft. He enters me and my head rolls back, exposing my neck to him.

I whisper his name, "Jackson…"

I feel as if the rest of the world has dropped away and there is no one and nothing else other than us, this precious intimacy, and connection between our bodies. The exquisite gentleness of his shaft entering me inch by inch makes me moan. His hand caresses my breast. My body moves and bows, but almost as if in slow motion. I feel it all—the passion, the desire, the throbbing need. His tongue probes my mouth as his thumb finds my clit and slowly circles it. I shiver with the sensation.

He is fully inside me now and we are both breathing hard.

"Oh, Jackson," I whisper again and again. Helpless to the wash of emotions and sensations filling my body.

I suck his on tongue, mindless with bliss, as he enters and withdraws out of me. Like the tide, the moment is smooth, relentless. It reminds of something that will last forever and ever. It's beyond beautiful.

Jackson tenses. I know what that means. "Don't stop. I'm nearly there," I breathe.

His thumb moves in faster circles, heightening the pleasure, as he continues to slowly slide in and out of me, each movement a finely tuned play of muscles, bone, and sinew. All of it for my pleasure. And the pleasure is intoxicating. I've never been this intimate with anyone before. His thumb moves steadily, patient but wanting something from me.

I begin to breathe deeper and faster. My hips push back against his, seeking him, reaching out for that gorgeous release. I feel his cock swell inside me, filling with blood, becoming harder and more insistent.

Gone are the slow, tender thrusts, the caresses, the hypnotic kisses, the vast control. What remains is a wild hunger that pounds into me. Intense, it pushes me over the edge. Inside that passionate, hungry embrace, my body begins to shake uncontrollably, but he doesn't stop, doesn't let up. Like the ocean he just keeps going, thrusting as deep as he can into me. An involuntary scream tears through me as I begin to soar—each breath that heaves out of me brings forth new ecstasy.

I'm shuddering, bucking, and spasming. Lost.

From far away, I hear him say my climax is the most beautiful thing he has ever seen. Then he gives into his own pleasure. Our tense bodies meld, we rock against each other, both desperate to make it last. We stay like that, locked together, Jackson inside me, as our orgasms slowly ease away. We want to hold the moment to us, but it ebbs away like morning dew.

He is first to speak, his voice full of awe, "That was so beautiful."

"I know," I whisper. "I didn't want it to be over."

His eyes fill with light. "There will be more. Many more."

"Promise?"

"Promise," he says softly.

I still can't believe what happened. "Nothing like that has ever happened to me before."

He looks deep into my eyes. "Me neither."

I touch his face tenderly. "I'm glad."

"Do you want to go back to sleep for a bit?"

"No, I have to go and check on Draco," I say, and

reluctantly pull myself away from him. "I need to feed him and give him his meds."

"You can bring him in here if you like?" he offers.

"Are you sure?"

He smiles gently. His face is still softened with the intensity of our coupling. "Of course, I'm sure. Tyrion will love the company. Why don't you go and do what you need to do and I'll start making some breakfast? We can take them both for a walk, after that."

"A short walk, though," I say. "Draco needs to start getting some exercise again, but the vet had said not to rush anything. Little by little." Talking about mundane things. helps bring me back down to earth. Slowly, the magic is easing, but it is not all quite gone.

"Okay," he says.

"Oh, and my Mom is coming by later. Just to warn you. You don't need to be around for it if you don't want to."

He smiles. "I'd love to see her again. Try and clear the air after last time… that was a little awkward."

I grin. "Yeah, it was more awkward for me, thank you! Standing there in my camisole which Mom thought was a top!"

"Um…I don't think so. I was hiding my hard-on with a cushion, remember?"

We both crack up thinking about it.

"That seems like such a long time ago," I say. I can't believe how nervous I'd been around him that evening.

"The night of the dreaded *lovecake*." He sniggers.

I punch him hard in his side.

"Okay, you'll pay for that." He lunges for me, but I'm too quick for him. I evade his hands, roll of the bed and end up falling on the floor. He looks down at me from the edge of the bed. "Are you all right?"

"Why wouldn't I be? I'm just going to do some push-ups," I say and start doing some push-ups.

He is still laughing as I pull on some leggings and a T-shirt. He stops though, when I tell him I can feel his cum running out of me.

I quickly run across to my place where Draco is eager to see me. "I know. I know. I've been leaving you alone too much. All that is going to stop now and I'm going to take you with me all the time now."

As if he understands he starts waging his tail furiously and making that almost purring sound he makes when he is very, very happy. I take him to the kitchen.

"Good boy, Draco," I coo, stroking his head, as he wolfs down his food. I'm glad his appetite is finally coming back after the op.

Then I give him his medication, grab his blanket, and take him back to Jackson's, from where delicious smells of bacon and eggs cooking waft into our noses. Draco's nose twitches away and I think maybe, he'll be allowed a tiny bit of bacon.

Just this once.

Chapter Forty-One

JACKSON

"Bye Mrs. Appleton. It was great to see you again." I smile, closing the door behind her.

"I hope that wasn't a sigh of relief," Lauren teases.

"Nah, your Mom's sweet in her own way," I say. "She talks a lot, though."

"You're going to think I had an ulterior motive for inviting her over here for afternoon tea," I tell her, kissing her on the forehead.

"Oh?" she says, narrowing her eyes. "Why's that?"

"Do you have any plans Saturday?"

"Why?" she asks, looking so suspicious it makes me laugh.

"It's nothing too awful, I promise! It's the annual Architect's ball. I have to go. It's a charity thing and it's going to be pretty dull, but it'll be a lot better if you came…"

"You want to take me with you?" she asks, a smile growing on her sweet lips.

"Yeah, I do."

The smile becomes full-blown. "I promised I'd help Danny out with some painting during the day, but I'm not doing anything in the evening so sure, I'd love to."

"Good. The food is always amazing and there's an open bar."

"Sounds great. What's the catch?"

"Well, we'll be sitting with my parents at dinner… and there'll be rather a lot of boring speeches and awards."

"I think I can handle that." She smiles. "Especially, if since say your Dad's been a bit more chill recently too."

"It's quite a fancy affair so you'll have to dress up. I don't know if you have anything like that but I'm happy to take you shopping if you don't?"

She smiles at me and touches my arm. "It's so sweet of you to offer, but you don't need to do that. I think I have just the thing… it's pretty sexy, though."

I'm curious now. "How so?"

"Well it's long, red, a little sparkly, it has a slit to somewhere in the middle of my left thigh, and its strapless." Suddenly, she looks unsure. "I hope your parents won't think it's too much?"

"Two things. A: It's sounds absolutely stunning. B: You're my girl, not my parent's." Then I start unbuttoning her blouse. "Did I hear you mention something about your left thigh?"

"I might have. Why?"

"Because my cock is already hard."

Chapter Forty-Two

LAUREN

"Nina isn't here yet?" I ask, giving Pam a big hug. She's wearing a long floaty skirt with a baby blue cashmere roll neck sweater, her shiny auburn hair skimming her shoulders. I take off my coat and slip into the seat next to her.

"No, I just got here. Managed to grab a table. I didn't realize how busy it gets in here. On a Monday, as well!"

"You've forgotten what city life is like, haven't you?" I tease.

She laughs. "Yeah, maybe you're right. It is a bit of a culture shock being back. Just seems so loud and so crowded here after being in such a remote place for so long."

"It must have been amazing," I say. "I've always wished I could see more of the world. And you've done it and managed to help out in the community there as well!"

"You have to come and visit," she says excitedly, putting her hand on mine. "David and I are planning to go back as soon as we can. You really feel like you're making a difference out there. And the people are so warm and lovely."

"See if you can stop me from coming to visit."

"Bring Jackson too, of course," she says. "I'm so glad you've found someone special."

I smile. "Yeah, I know, he is pretty beautiful isn't he! I was surprised he even noticed me, let alone wanted to go out with me."

"Lolly, stop that!" she scolds. "You're every inch as beautiful as he is. More if you ask me."

"I've missed you," I tell her. "And I can't believe you're getting married."

"I know!" she says, her eyes shining.

"So, when do we get to meet him? I mean, it's quite ridiculous that we haven't already."

"I know, I'm sorry. He's just so busy with work and stuff. We've actually not spent much time together recently, at all. He's been back and forth trying to sort out his business. And he's got his bachelor party this weekend even though the wedding's not for another two months!"

"Next weekend?" I say, "That's funny, Jackson was meant to be going to Tahoe on a bachelor party then too, but he can't go now."

"Well, I was going to suggest we get away for a kind of bachelorette thing…" she suggests, "I don't want anything crazy. Just the four of us girls and maybe a couple of my old work friends."

"Count me in!" I say. "But you're not talking about this weekend, are you?"

"I figured you guys would probably be busy at such late notice," she says. "I'm sorry I didn't get in touch more regularly. But the internet is so flaky out there. We're lucky even to have power sometimes!"

"That's ok," I grin. "I totally understand. And let me organize something for you. Please?"

"Would you really?" she asks me, looking all coy.

"Where do you want to go?" I ask.

"I don't know… I was thinking maybe a nice spa place around Napa, so we can go wine tasting too."

"Sounds awesome."

"And don't worry about the money," she continues. "David wants to treat us! I think he feels bad about keeping me away from you guys for so long!"

"Hey! Sorry I'm late you guys!" Nina yells, hugging Pam, then me and sitting down with us.

We catch up on her most recent date, who turns out to be lacking in several departments according to Nina, and then turn to talk of the spa weekend away.

"Oh my God, this is going to be so much fun!" Nina squeals. "But why don't we go this weekend when David's away too?"

"I can't," I say. "I'm sorry. I already said I'd go to this architect ball thing with Jackson and his folks."

"Ooh, things are getting serious with you two, Lolly." Nina grins.

I tell her to shut up. "How about the weekend after instead?" I suggest. "I'll text Andrea."

"Yeah, where is she, anyway?" Pam asks.

"Probably with Ricardo!" I reply. "They seem to be seeing a lot of each other recently."

"Ugh. Everyone's loved up except me!" Nina complains. "It's not fair!"

"Aw, there'll be someone for you!" Pam reassures her.

And suddenly, I have an idea.

Chapter Forty-Three

JACKSON

When I inform Joe that I'm not going to the Tahoe weekend and he finally got it that I wasn't going, he really blew his cool. Accusing me of choosing a woman over the guy's, saying that ever since I met Lauren I have had even less time to spend with the guys. He even hung up on me.

I decide to walk back to my place from work to calm down. I'm striding up and down streets, marching out my aggression. What the hell, Joe? When are you ever going to grow the hell up?

I notice a figure up ahead and I recognize him immediately. That idiot from Lauren's work. The image of his hand on the small of Lauren's back flashes in my head. That wasn't a man taking his colleague out to dinner, that was a man on the hunt.

Almost instantly, I feel the blood rushing to my brain. My fists curl and tighten into ball hammers of pure fury. I know men like him. They don't respect boundaries and I don't buy that bullshit story he sold Lauren about being cheated by his ex. Men, like him. They do the cheating.

Despite the red haze in my brain, I would have walked past him and not said anything, but as luck would have it, he is a psychopath who has to have his pound of flesh.

He's quite well built, but I'm bigger and I'm pretty sure stronger than him. He picked the wrong guy to play his games with.

"Don't I know you?" he asks, a self-satisfied smirk on his face that I am dying to punch out.

"No, and you don't want to know me," I tell him, aggressively.

"Chill man. It's a beautiful day."

Yeah, the perfect day to knock your lights out. "Keep away from Lauren. Or you'll regret it."

His eyes widen as he realizes how he knows me. "Are you threatening me?" he asks.

I can see he's no longer sure of himself. I'm wearing a suit, but inside I'm all caveman. He didn't expect that. "Yeah, I am. Do you understand?"

I'm towering over him, glowering at him. I can see he's intimidated.

I keep on staring him down and unconsciously he starts backing away. "Yeah sure. Sorry. We just work together. It was nothing," he mumbles.

"It better be nothing. I see you touch her again and I'll break your hand," I threaten menacingly.

"Yeah, man. Sure."

I watch the little coward walking hurriedly away from me, glancing back a few times. It is a long time before my fists uncurl and my breathing returns to normal. Lauren is mine and the sooner everybody understands that, the better life will be for them.

Chapter Forty-Four

LAUREN

"Hey, Matthew," I greet cheerfully, as I get into the office. No matter what time I get in, he always seems to be there before me.

"Hey," he replies, not looking up from his computer.

"Everything all right?" I ask him.

He just nods and continues typing.

Okay. I shrug and settle into my new desk. I'm loving my new position already. I log on to my computer and check what's on the schedule for today. I can't believe how much my life has transformed in the last couple of weeks, but while my career advancement has put a spring in my step, it's Jackson who's made my heart sing. I smile just thinking about him, but then I get a nervous twist in my stomach when I think of the big architect's ball coming up on Saturday. I just hope I don't let him down.

"Lauren, have you finished the prep for the site visit tomorrow?" Matthew asks sternly.

I look up at him, confused. "I only just got in… I'll get it done straight away."

"Make sure you do," he says, and wanders off.

Jeez, I wonder what's up with him. I quickly open the file he's talking about and start reading through the documents.

Lunchtime comes and goes and I'm still working on it, munching on a sandwich at my desk. Finally, I think it's done and I sigh with relief and leave it on Matthew's desk for him to look over before I take it my team to start working on it.

Going to my table, I sip on my green juice and open the browser on my computer to search for spa hotels around Napa. I cringe at some of the prices and wonder how much this fiancée of Pam's is willing to spend on us. He's already shelling out for all our bridesmaid's dresses, hair, and makeup on the day. What a guy!

"That doesn't look like work," Matthew tuts as he walks past my desk.

"Oh, sorry!" I say, surprised that he would say something. Maybe I should have brought my Do Not Disturb sign with me, I think to myself. "I worked through my lunch to get that site survey prep done so I didn't think it would be a problem. The report is on your desk."

He walks off without a reply.

Chapter Forty-Five

LAUREN

"I just don't understand," I wail to Andrea. "Things were going so well!"

"I don't understand, either." She frowns. "But you need to talk to him about it. It's not fair on you. You at least deserve an explanation."

"He told me I'm not fulfilling my responsibilities. That maybe I'm not ready for the role. He's going to suggest to Mr. Montfort that one of the other members of the team might be more suitable to lead."

"That's ridiculous," she snorts. "You're one of the most intelligent women I know. You told me you're working your ass off there and I believe you. I have no doubt that you're doing great."

"Thanks," I mutter. "What would you do if you were me?"

She considers this for a moment and then says, "Could there be any other reason? Do you think it's because you rejected him?"

"I wouldn't say I rejected him. I just said made it clear I wanted to keep our relationship purely professional. It didn't seem to bother him at all." I think back to that night and sincerely hope I'm remembering it correctly. Could he have been expecting us to become more than friends? But that didn't make sense because he had literally turned cold overnight.

"Men can be strange creatures," Andrea eventually says, sipping on her soy chai latte, and then glancing at her phone for about the seventh time that evening.

"Are you waiting to hear from someone?" I ask, narrowing my eyes. This behavior was most unlike ice queen Andrea. "Ricardo not texting you?"

She glowers at me and refutes the idea immediately. "As if," she huffs, then nonchalantly throws her phone in her bag.

I know better than to delve so I move on quickly, "So anyway, before Matthew got all weird the last couple of days, I was actually thinking about setting him up with Nina."

"Wouldn't that be a bit off, given your history?" she asks, accusingly.

"For goodness sake, nothing happened between us. Mathew and I had dinner together after working flat out for a whole afternoon. End of story."

She smirks. "I know, Laurie. As if you'd do anything so exciting!"

I lower my head. "Laugh all you want, but at that time I had already fallen for Jackson. I was even scared about liking him too much so doing anything with Mathew or any other man didn't even cross my mind," I admit.

"Why should you be scared about liking someone?" she asks curiously.

I look up at her. "For the same reason you're scared of liking Ricardo too much."

She looks away. I don't speak and after a while, she

turns her face back to me. "Ricardo's not answering my texts," she says, her voice quivering slightly.

"Oh, babe," I say, my heart sinking for her. "He'll be in touch soon. I cannot believe he won't. You are such a catch. When has any man dropped you?"

She bites her lip. "There's always the first time. And of course, it would have to happened with a guy I really like."

"When did you last hear from him?"

"Monday," she whispered. Her eyes glaze over for a second and then she focuses on me again. "We went to yoga, dropped in to see Danny, then had an amazing dinner at this new rooftop place his friend owns. Amazing sex in the hot tub too afterwards… and then nothing."

"It doesn't sound like you have anything to worry about," I say, feeling more envy than pity for her. Sex in a hot tub, wow.

"I sent him a text the next morning, but I haven't heard anything back."

"You haven't messaged him since then?"

She shakes her head and I'm amazed at her will power.

"Anyway," she says, sitting up straight. "It's only what I've done to so many men in the past. So, I suppose it serves me right!" She grins. "And where the hell is Nina?" she asks, looking around. "We need to get this bachelorette party organized!"

"She'll be here soon, you know she's always late! And anyway, I want to hear more about this hot tub."

Chapter Forty-Six

JACKSON

I hear the knock on the door and jump up to let her in. "How was dinner, gorgeous?" I ask her. And she does look gorgeous. Mind-blowingly gorgeous. Her skin fresh and natural, without make-up. Her hair pulled back in a braid, with loose strands framing her beautiful face.

"Great," she says, hugging me tight and kissing me. "What did you get up to tonight?"

"Just work, the usual shit. But anyway. You're here now." I pick her up and lay her down on the sofa. She's giggling as I do.

"Drink?" I could do with one tonight."

"I think I'll just have a cup of a tea, actually. I need to get an early night. I don't know what I've done but Matthew is making my life hell at the moment. Everything I do isn't good enough and he got funny with me for being on the internet on my lunch break."

Shit. I remember my little encounter with Matthew on Monday night.

"And he's been hinting that I'm not up to the job.

Which is so weird because only day before yesterday he said, I was a natural. To top it all off, I've never worked so hard in my life. It's so frustrating." I sigh. "I think he's going to recommend to Mr. Montfort to ask for someone else to lead the team. Which will be a blow for me, but there's not a damned thing I can do about it."

"No!" I say. "That's not fair. You're great at your job. And that project is your baby."

"Yeah," she says with a heavy sigh, "but if Mr. Montfort gets involved, I could even be kept out of the project. It's as simple as that."

I hesitate. I'm going to have to sort this out. Should I tell her? I can't believe I might have jeopardized her career. What an idiot I am. Fuck, instead of punching him I should punch myself.

"What are you thinking about?" she asks me, looking confused.

I stand and put the kettle on to boil, then I sit down next to her on the sofa. "I did something really stupid and I'm really sorry," I tell her, watching with dismay as the confusion on her face grows. "I saw Matthew on the street. I can't remember exactly what I said now, because I was so angry, but basically, I warned him to stay away from you. I'm so sorry."

"What?" she says, her mouth dropping open. "You did what?"

I take her hands in mine.

She pulls away. "Here I was thinking I'd done something wrong or I was shit at my job!" she cries out, glaring at me.

"Lauren, I'm sorry. I was going to walk past, I swear, but then he stopped me and asked me something and he had this stupid gloating smile on him. When I saw it, I just saw red. How dare he take my girl out for dinner? *I* was going to take you to that nice Italian place in the Marina."

Her eyes soften a little. "You can still take me there," she says quietly. "But you'll have to apologize to Matthew first."

"I'm not apologizing to that little jerk. I know his kind. He can lie to you all he wants I know he wants to fuck you," I say, feeling the blood rise to my head. There was no way I was saying sorry to him.

She's looking at me, waiting, defiance in her eyes. "I could lose my job over this. And all you care about is your ego." She shakes her head in disgust and she gets up in a huff. "I think I'll sleep at my place tonight."

I don't try to stop her. I'm too angry with him and myself.

Fuck, fuck, fuck.

Chapter Forty-Seven

LAUREN

I'm up early after a night of not much sleep, sitting on the sofa with Draco and a cup of coffee.

"Aw, Draco, why is everything so complicated?" I ask him, looking into his wise old eyes. I swear if he could talk, he'd give me the best advice ever.

Danny walks in and stops in his tracks. "I don't think I've ever seen you up this early," he jokes.

"I couldn't sleep." I give Draco a tummy rub.

"Weren't you at Jackson's last night?"

"Nah… We had a bit of an argument." I tell him what happened and how Matthew had been behaving so differently towards me. "Do you think it's because of what Jackson said to him?"

"What Jackson did is not cool," he replies frowning. "Whether it's got anything to do with Matthew's attitude towards you or not. Do you think it could be because he's interested in you?" he adds.

"I doubt it. I really don't think he's in love with me or anything like that. He was completely cool with it until Jackson put his oar in it."

"I think you just need to talk to him. Why don't you go in early and see if you can catch him alone?"

"Yeah, that's what I was thinking," I say, "I'm really pissed that Jackson won't apologize though."

"Male ego," Danny says immediately. "And you can't blame him for wanting to mark his property, either."

"Ew, don't say that," I say, frowning at him. "I'm not his property. You make him sound like a dog peeing on me."

We both burst out laughing but inside, I'm still miffed about Jackson's behavior. I'm tempted to go and see him before work, but I want to get things with Matthew sorted first.

Chapter Forty-Eight

LAUREN

Dreading having the conversation with him, I gingerly walk into the office and glance around. I'm the first one in, even before Mathew and no one gets in before him. I dump my bag and coat at my desk and go to the kitchenette to put on some coffee.

"Oh, hey! Good morning!" I say, extra cheerfully, when he walks into the kitchen a few minutes later. I'm so jittery I almost spill the coffee. "Would you like some?"

"Um, yes, sure," he says, obviously surprised to see me. "You're in extra early."

"Yeah, I wanted to catch you actually. Before anyone else got in. I hoped we could clear the air."

"Oh?"

"Yeah, I was really disappointed when you told me I haven't been pulling my weight around here. I've been trying so hard." I quickly blink back the tears that are threatening to escape and take a deep breath, waiting for his reply.

I'm surprised when he touches me kindly on the shoulder. "Lauren, I'm so sorry." His voice is quiet and sincere.

"I know I've been in a bad mood this week and I apologize for letting my personal affairs affect me professionally."

I look at him and notice the tiredness and angst in his eyes. "Personal affairs?" I ask quietly, not knowing whether I should or not.

He stares at the floor for a moment.

"It's ok if you'd rather not tell me," I add. "I don't want to pry."

"No, it's fine," he says, shaking his head and making eye contact with me again. His normally clean-shaven jaw is covered with blonde stubble. "It's my ex. When I got home Monday night, I found the custody papers she sent me. She wants full custody of our son. She wants to take him away from me."

"Oh God, I'm so sorry!"

"It's ok. I spoke to my lawyer last night and she thinks we have a pretty good case so it should be ok. But it really freaked me out, thinking she might be able to take him away from me."

"I really hope it all works out for you." I can't imagine what he must be going through right now. And here I am, wrapped up in my own silly problems, as usual.

He smiles. "Yeah, me too. But I'm really sorry for being grumpy with you." He pauses. "And I had an awkward encounter with your aggressive boyfriend too, telling me to back off. I'm sorry Lauren. I've just had so much going on in my head the last couple of days. I know you've been doing a good job."

"It's ok, I understand," I say, smiling, although my blood is boiling thinking about Jackson bullying a man who is under so much stress.

"You have no need to worry about your position in this team. Your work has been excellent. The report you finished yesterday was far more thorough than anyone else usually manages. I was very impressed. I shouldn't have let anyone else affect my opinion of you."

"Thanks," I say, the relief flooding through me.

"So as long as you continue to do so well, as far as I'm concerned you are the leader of this team for as long as you want."

"Really? That's fantastic. Thank you so much!" My heart is pounding. I can't believe the good news.

"I'm really glad you came in early so we could talk about this," he continues. "I was planning to pull you aside today and have a chat. I felt really bad about snapping at you."

"And I'm really sorry about Jackson," I say. "He got funny about seeing us out together the other night, but I had no idea he would accost you like that in the street!"

"Oh, don't worry about that. Didn't he tell you? He got in contact with me last night. Found me on our company Facebook page. He apologized. Asked me if I wanted to come along to softball sometime."

This is news to me. My heart starts singing. Maybe I'd overreacted when I'd stormed out of his house last night, but maybe that's what it took to get him to say sorry. Tough love worked this time. "He's a really nice guy, most of the time," I assure him. "I'm sure you two will get along. Just a bit protective I guess."

"I can understand why," he says, grinning. "And I'm not saying that in a creepy way. Yes, you're gorgeous, but you're also a genuine caring person. Not to mention hard-working and intelligent too."

I can feel my cheeks getting hot and I look away. "Um, thanks. Another cup of coffee?"

He's laughing. "Although you should really work on accepting compliments better. Look, I know things got a little… flirty, shall we say, that night after our first day working together. But if I'm honest, that was purely the booze talking. You're not really my type."

I grin back, incredibly relieved. "I'm just glad we've sorted things out," I say. "It was really worrying me, but to know you think I'm doing a good job is all I wanted to hear."

"You are." He grins again. "So keep up the good work."

"I will, but on another note... what is your type?"

He laughs. "Petite. Long dark hair. Dark eyes. I guess... Why, you have anyone in mind?"

"Maybe," I reply, raising my eyebrows and smiling.

"I see..." He grins, then holds out his coffee cup for me to top off.

Chapter Forty-Nine

LAUREN

"So, no Friday night cocktails tonight, girls? What's the world coming to?" Danny says to Andrea and I, as we lounge on the couch at my place. "Not that I'm complaining, though," he adds, "How do you like the kombucha?"

"It's interesting…" Andrea says, taking a sip.

"I like it. But I'm not sure I'd swap it for cocktails every Friday night." I give Danny a wink.

"Enjoy me while you can," Andrea says. "I'm being picked up soon."

"Oh?" I ask.

She grins. "Yeah, Ricardo. He left his phone in an Uber and then he was travelling for work. Hence the radio silence!"

"I knew there'd be an explanation," I cry out. "I hope he made it up to you."

"Yeah… you could say that," she says with one of cat got the cream expressions.

"Not more hot tub antics?" Danny teases her.

She gives me a look.

"I didn't think it was a secret!" I protest.

"She's just jealous." Danny chuckles. "She's been having sexy hot tub dreams about her and Jackson ever since you told her that story."

"Oi!" I say, but Danny and Andrea are laughing their asses off.

"Haven't you ever had sex in a hot tub before?" Andrea asks me.

I shake my head, feeling like the most innocent person alive. "So, are you going to take Ricardo as your plus one to Pam's wedding?" I ask her.

"Oh, I don't know, that's months away yet. Where's Nina tonight, anyway?"

"You two are really good at avoiding questions you don't want to answer," Danny observes. "But yeah, but where is the lovely Nina?"

"On a date," I say, mysteriously.

"Surprise, surprise," Andrea remarks, smiling. "Who's the unfortunate man tonight who we're going to hear picked apart tomorrow, then?"

"I hope that won't be the case," I say, "It might be a little awkward. She's on a date with Matthew."

"Oh, you set them up. How fun!" Danny beams, clapping his hands.

"Well, I'll look forward to hearing how that goes," Andrea says. Her phone pings at that moment and I see her eyes light up. "Better go," she says. "He's here."

We wave her off and settle back down on the couch. I pat the empty space she's left for Draco to come and join us then give him a little help as he struggles to make it up.

"Aw poor Draco," Danny says, giving him a rub.

"He's doing really well, actually. We took him on a nice

slow walk this morning before work. He even had a bit of a jog at the end of it."

Draco turns on his back and Danny rubs his stomach too. "No wonder you're tired old boy." He looks up at me. "So, you made up with Jackson, then?"

"Yes," I say, beaming with relief. "He apologized to Matthew. We hung out last night after he played softball. He said sorry for being an idiot. And look what he sent me at work today!" I reach into my bag and take out the little box of artisan heart-shaped Belgian dark chocolates.

Danny coos at the beautiful little box and then reads the card attached:

My beautiful AP. Pack your toothbrush for tomorrow night ;)
Love JS xx.
Ps. Sorry again for being an idiot!

"I thought you were going to a ball tomorrow?"

"I guess we're staying somewhere after this ball thing with his folks. I'll be packing more than just a toothbrush if that's the case."

"Oh, how romantic!" Danny says dreamily.

"I suppose it is, but I'm getting more and more nervous about tomorrow night though."

"You'll be fine."

"I guess… well, I think I'm going to get an early night anyway. What time do you want to leave tomorrow morning?

"Around nine?" he says tentatively.

"Oh yeah, that's fine. I was worried you were going to say six o'clock or something."

He rubs his hands together. "Nah, we're nearly there. Not long until the grand opening now."

"I'm so proud of you," I tell him, giving him a hug over Draco who's now snoring softly. "It's such an achievement and you did it all by yourself!"

"I had a lot of help. A great team of volunteers. And of course, we've got Andrea to thank for the final influx of cash."

"Not such a bad person after all," I say, winking.

He grins. "Yeah, you're right. I got her wrong. I just didn't know her well enough, I guess."

"Well, I think Ricardo has been a good influence too. Softened her up a bit!"

"Yeah, I want to meet this mystery man!"

"Me too. I hope she brings him to the wedding."

"Aw, I wish I was going," he says, pulling a face.

I'm disappointed that Pam didn't invite him. "She wanted to so much but they're so tight on numbers and they had to draw the line somewhere," I say, touching his arm.

"It's ok. I understand. I do love a good wedding though," he says, grinning.

"We're going to get our bridesmaids dresses fitted next week. They're so pretty. I can't wait."

"You girls are going to look amazing. Now stop rubbing it in."

"Sorry darling. Anyway, I'm sure we'll meet Ricardo before then. Andrea did say she might bring him out one Friday night with us."

"I hope so. She's so elusive about him."

"I know! But I did get a glimpse of him the other night. He dropped her off when we met for dinner on Wednesday."

"What did you see?"

"He was wearing a suit and sunglasses so hard to say,

but was tall and had a very confident air about him. Sort of a swagger to him, if you know what I mean. And he was driving a really fancy car. Bentley, I think."

"That figures." Danny sniggers. "She's got expensive taste, that one."

Chapter Fifty

LAUREN

We pile back into my house after a busy afternoon of painting at Danny's project.

"Thanks, everyone," Danny yells. "You guys are the best! And special thanks to Jackson who did the majority of the work. Those muscles, wow!"

"Hey!" I exclaim. "Andrea and I worked just as hard!"

"But we don't look as good in a tight T-shirt," Andrea says, winking and looking over to Jackson.

He had just turned up to help, which made me feel proud, happy and grateful. I laugh, "Oh, Danny, is it true?" I tease him.

He turns a little pink and says, with a grin. "Of course not. Don't be ridiculous!"

"Glad to hear I'm not just a sex object!" Jackson says, putting his hands on his hips and looking *exactly* like a sex object. He looked exceptionally sexy today, his tight t-shirt and ample biceps splattered with white paint. So deliciously blue collar, working man, delectable.

"Oh, you're definitely *my* sex object," I say, and Andrea groans audibly in the background.

Jackson winks at me then moves forward to shake Danny's hand. "I'm gonna head back to my place for a bit. I need to wash this paint off me before tonight. Good luck, man."

"Thanks again, dude," Danny responds, as he enthusiastically pumps his hand.

Jackson turns to me and brushes his lips against my forehead. "I'll pick you up at seven, gorgeous."

I check my phone. "It's five-thirty already. Shit, I need to get moving."

"Me too," Andrea agrees, with a wicked look in her eyes.

"Ricardo?" I ask.

She nods slyly, blows me a kiss and is out of the door before I can ask any more questions.

"Can't believe what a dark horse she turned out to be," I say to Danny.

"Yeah, speaking of dark horses," he says. "I've decided to end it with Feather."

"Oh, no, I'm sorry. How come?"

"When I found out she stole the cupcake with the love potion, at first I thought it was funny. But when I thought about it a bit more, I was shocked."

"I did think it was a bit... shady," I say gently.

"A bit shady? She stole from you! Something which was worth four hundred dollars at the least, and possibly love at the most. For selfish reasons, too. I take it she didn't offer to give you the money back?"

I shake my head.

"And her not turning up today was the final straw," he says, and then pauses. "Well, that and the sex wasn't really doing it for me anymore either..."

"I *was* a little surprised," I say to him. "I was wondering if maybe she did give the lovecake to you after all."

"Oh, God, can you imagine?" he cracks up. "How dreadful!

"But you weren't being very subtle about lusting over Jackson, so I guess that proves it."

"Oh, I've definitely still got it, darling." he winks and grabs his phone. Scrolls through the messages until the name Darren *Handyman* comes up, the new maintenance guy for our building, with a message far saucier than I ever would have given him credit for!

"Danny and Darren, eh?" I say, smiling. "He is cute, I'll give you that." I suddenly glance at my phone. "Eek, it's almost six."

"So…" Danny yells, running to my bedroom. "It's the night for Jessica Rabbit to come out." He flings open my wardrobe doors and pulls out the gorgeous dazzling red number. "Oh wow," he mutters. "I can't wait to see you in this incredible get up."

"Yeah," I say. "I can't believe I've finally got a chance to wear it."

"What bag?" he asks. "And which shoes?" He starts rummaging through my wardrobe, discarding items on the floor. A boot comes flying out and I move to avoid it. He turns to look at me. "What are you standing there for? Go and shower and I'll sort out the accessories," he orders.

I nod and jump to it.

Chapter Fifty-One

JACKSON

It's just before seven but I can't wait any longer. I can't wait to see her in the dress with the slit that stops in the middle of her left thigh. I straighten my jacket in the mirror and study my reflection. Not too bad. Then I slam the door behind me and hurry over to hers.

"Hey," I say to Danny as he swings open the door.

"I hope you're ready for her," he says with a wide grin.

"I am."

"Grid your loin man. You're not going to want her out of your sight tonight, that's for sure."

When I see her, I know what he means. She's a vision in red. The dress hugs her beautiful curves in the most amazing way. There is just enough cleavage without being slutty. As she walks towards me, the dress floats open at the side. The slit revealing one of her beautiful long legs, her feet are encased in dainty silver heels. She looks like…

"Wow," I say. "Wow!" It's all I can manage to utter right then.

She giggles, blushing. Her face unforgettable. A camera in my head snaps that moment. She will live forever in my head in this perfect moment. The dress, the hair, the shoes, the slit, the innocent look in her eyes.

"Not too much, is it?" she asks, twirling in front of me.

"You look… unbelievable." I take her hand and pull her towards me, kissing her full on the lips.

She kisses me back and we stand there just staring into each other's eyes.

"You look unbelievable too," she whispers in my ear. Then she raises her chin and nibbles my ear lobe. Hell, it makes me want to take her straight to bed. My mind wanders to thoughts of the hotel room I've booked for tonight and I'm wishing we could skip the damn ball and head straight there.

"Don't mind me," Danny teases.

We both remember and turn to look at him. He's laughing softly. He's a cool guy, I think. Lauren's lucky to have a friend and roommate like him.

Danny makes a shooing movement with his hands. "Go on. Take Jessica Rabbit to the ball."

Jessica Rabbit. Yes, Lauren Appleton is Jessica Rabbit in disguise.

I check my watch. "I guess we should go… although I don't really want to go anywhere with you looking like this. I'd rather keep you to myself."

She grins. "Don't you dare after all the effort Danny put into my appearance."

"True," I murmur. "We better get out of here then. Are you ready?"

She grabs her purse and a small overnight bag which I take from her.

"Wait!" Danny yells as we make towards the door. "I want a photo of the gorgeous couple!"

I don't tell him I've already taken a photograph—one that will last forever.

Chapter Fifty-Two

LAUREN

Despite all Jackson's efforts to calm me down on the way to the ball, I'm still feeling anxious when we arrive at the venue. We walk arm in arm through the grand entrance of the Fairmont Hotel.

"Have you ever been here before?" he asks.

"Once," I say, looking around the huge lobby in awe. "But only because Nina was dying to go for a pee after we'd been drinking in a bar down the street."

He laughs. "It's pretty spectacular, isn't it?"

"Yeah, from what I remember, the restrooms were bigger than my whole house."

"Wait till you see the rooms," he says, winking.

"Are we staying here?" I ask wide-eyed, as I follow him towards the elevators.

"We are," he drawls, and presses one of the buttons on the panel.

I feel a flutter in my stomach as we wait for it to ascend. Down a long corridor, he pulls a room card from his pocket and swipes it across the reader on one of the dark wood doors. The light turns green and he opens it wide for me.

"After you, my Miss Appleton."

All I can do is gasp as I look around the suite. It's ridiculously huge and extravagant. We're standing in the living room, full of regal armchairs, a luxurious leather couch, a beautiful rug adorning the floor and a chandelier hanging from the ceiling.

Jackson opens another door which leads to an equally huge bedroom.

I gasp with delight. The luxurious bed is covered in red rose petals and there is a fresh bouquet of roses next to the bed too, giving off an exquisite scent. He puts my bag on a shelf next to his and I realize he must have checked in earlier, while I was getting ready.

"Like it?"

"It's unbelievable!" I gush, looking up at him. "I love it. Are we really staying here tonight?"

"I figured we may as well make a night of it. And day… I've arranged a late check out tomorrow. I thought we could make use of the spa."

"This is amazing. Thank you so much, Jackson. You really didn't need to do this. We could have just gone back to your house afterwards, it's not exactly far, and I would have loved it just as much." The cab ride had lasted all of fifteen minutes.

He pulls me towards him and kisses me, looking deep into my eyes, making my heart melt. "I wanted to. I wanted to do something special for you. To say thank you for coming. And to make up for being an idiot about the whole Matthew thing."

I laugh. "Ah, in that case… please feel free to mess up again if this is how you make it up to me."

He beams, then checks his watch. "Pre-dinner cocktails

are at eight. We shouldn't be late. But we have just enough time to enjoy the view from the balcony."

"Balcony?"

But he's already taken my hand, and leading me back to the living room. He pulls the heavy curtains back to reveal beautiful cast-iron French windows which he opens wide. "Here," he says, draping a plush blanket over my shoulders.

I follow him out and we're greeted with the most wonderful view of the city. The night lights are sparkling and we can see all the way to Fisherman's Wharf and the Golden Gate Bridge.

A bottle of champagne on ice is waiting for us on the table with two glasses and he pops it open with a quiet hiss, then pouring the delicious fizzy liquid into the champagne flutes.

I hug the blanket around me in the cool evening breeze and take the glass he hands to me. I look up at him and smile. This has got to be the best date ever!

"To us," he says, his gorgeous eyes twinkling, dimples out in full force.

"To us," I echo quietly. I love him so much it feels as if my heart will burst.

We clink and drink. I savor the delicate taste, the bubbles fizzing in my throat. He puts his arm around me and we take in the breathtaking view.

Standing here in contented silence…I couldn't be happier.

Chapter Fifty-Three

JACKSON

I check my watch, but we still have a few moments alone before we need to join the party.

"I haven't seen you wearing this watch before," she says, admiring it, touching it with her delicate fingers.

"It's my grandfather's. I only wear it for my father's sake."

"It's beautiful." Her eyes are shining with excitement.

I'm glad my surprise has gone down well. She looks unbelievably beautiful tonight and I'm so proud to be taking her as my date. Although, I have to admit, I wish we could skip the ball altogether.

"What are you thinking?" she asks, smiling up at me.

"Just that I wish we could stay here all night, just you and me. Order room service and more champagne…"

"That does sound amazing." She giggles. "But I think your Dad would kill you. And me too, probably."

"You're right there," I nod, grinning at how well she knows my Dad already. "But we'll have plenty of time here alone later and tomorrow."

"I'm ready when you are," she says, sipping the last of her champagne.

"One more thing," I say and when she looks up at me again, I wrap my arms around her slender figure and kiss her softly. The kiss gets deeper and my cock gets harder. Now I know it's definitely time to leave. I take her hand to lead her back to the elevator and up to the top floor.

There's already a crowd of people milling around outside the main room, drinking champagne, chatting, nibbling on canapés. I glance around but I can't see my parents. A waiter approaches us with a tray and I take two champagne flutes, handing one to Lauren.

She smiles and thanks me, but her hand shakes.

"Are you nervous?" I ask her.

"Yeah, a little," she admits. "I've never been to such a glamorous event. Everyone looks so…amazing."

"No-one looks as good as you," I whisper and it's true. She's the most stunning woman here and I can feel people looking at us already.

"Jackson! Lauren!"

It's Mom. She hugs me and then Lauren, beaming at us. "Oh, Lauren you look stunning," she compliments. "Now come with me and I'll show you to our table. Jackson, your father is preparing for his speech but he'll be with us shortly."

I squeeze Lauren's hand as we make our way through clusters of smiling chatting people to the main room where the round tables are slowly filling.

"Here we are," she says as we get to one by the window. We find the place settings with our names and take a seat.

Chapter Fifty-Four

LAUREN

I gaze around the room, still taking all of it in. At the tables decorated with floral center pieces, at the massive chandelier, the waiters gliding by, the flamboyant outfits in the room, at the cards explaining that it's been 110 years since the hotel opened its doors to guests for the first time, along with some other historical facts about the place. I'm glad these things distract me from the monotonous speeches.

Dessert is brought to our table. Delicate filo pastry parcels filled with rich gooey dark chocolate with a tiny jug of caramel sauce to pour over the top. And finally, there's a round of applause as the last speech is over.

"I hope it wasn't too boring for you, Lauren," Jackson's Mom says to me.

"Oh no, not at all. I've enjoyed the evening, thank you."

His Dad starts laughing. Jackson was right, the change in him is astounding. He's been charming all night. "You don't need to humor us," he says, grinning, his eyes twinkling just like Jackson's. "I'm sure there are a hundred places you'd rather be tonight!"

I smile. He's trying to put me on the spot. "I wouldn't say that," I protest. "It's not often I get the chance to dress up and come to such a beautiful place. Some of the speeches were a little…well, long, but yours I very much enjoyed. And the food has been fantastic."

I take a spoonful of desert as if to prove my point.

"I see," his Dad continues. "And what, if I may ask, did you particularly enjoy about my speech?"

I rack my brain trying to remember something notable. But all I can think of is how proudly he spoke of the industry and in regards to Jackson. "I just thought it was very heartfelt and genuine."

"It was, Dad. It was great," Jackson interjects.

I squeeze Jackson's leg under the table for coming to my rescue, and he smiles indulgently at me.

"So, did David forgive you for not going to Tahoe?" his Mom asks.

He laughs. "It was Joe who was the main problem. He is still mad at me for ruining his party, David was cool about it. We sorted it out. He understood."

"I'm looking forward to meeting the mysterious Pamela," his mother says.

This got my attention. Pamela? And Pam's bridegroom is called David. It can't be… Surely not. "Hang on a minute," I interject. "Pamela?"

"Yes, David met her in Africa, isn't that right, Jackson?"

"What's the date of the wedding?" I ask, my brain whirring away.

Jackson's looking at me, confused. Then he clicks. "Your friend, Pam? No way! It's… umm."

"It's on the 6th," his Mom finishes for him, and then turns to me in surprise. "Do you know Pamela, Lauren?"

"I can't believe it," I say. "Yes, it must be the same Pamela and David."

"This is crazy," Jackson says, shaking his head, laughing.

"She's been one of my best friends since high school," I explain to his parents. "I'm going to be one of her bridesmaids."

"So I guess you didn't need to invite Lauren, after all!" His dad says with a laugh. "She's a more important guest than you."

"It means I can take Danny as my plus one instead of you," I tell Jackson, winking. I can't wait to text Pam and tell her the strange coincidence.

We file out of the room after dinner, back to the hall where we started the evening. There's a bar at one end and a band at the other. They start playing some old songs from the sixties, music that reminds me of my childhood.

"Wanna dance?" Jackson asks me.

I don't know if I can still remember how to waltz, but I nod.

He takes my hand, leads me to the middle of the floor where other couples are swaying. His arm wraps around my waist and mine around his shoulders. Then he twirls me away. It is like a dream. Looking into his eyes, I couldn't be happier.

"Your Dad's like a different person," I say to Jackson.

"I know, I'm so glad he's happier. For Mom's sake more than anything."

I giggle. "I know all about difficult fathers! You'll have to meet my Dad soon."

"I'd love to. You don't talk about him very much."

"I guess I'm closer to my Mom. Dad always wanted a son I think."

"Aw, how wrong he was. You're perfect. I'm sure he would have been proud of you tonight. You look amazing!"

I smile. "I'm glad everyone else is really dressed up too. I was worried everyone would be looking at me."

"Oh, they were." He winks at me. "Every single guy in the room was jealous of me tonight."

"Stop it!" I hit him playfully, trying to not blush.

"Let's go get a cocktail," he says as the song comes to an end.

His parents are at the bar, smiling at us and to my amusement Jackson looks a little embarrassed.

We say our goodbyes and wave them off, and as soon as they're out of sight, Jackson turns to me then kisses me long and deep, hugging me tight. "Shall we get out of here?"

I nod. I've been longing to be alone with him again!

We slip out of the venue and back upstairs to our beautiful room where more flowers have been delivered and a fresh bottle of champagne is awaiting us in the living room. Jackson pops it open and we toast to a successful night. To be honest, I'm a little relieved it's all over, although it was much better than I'd expected.

He catches my hand, pulling me towards him. He strokes my face, and looking deep into my eyes, captures my lips in a fiery kiss. Then when he pulls his lips from mine, he states, "I am the luckiest man in the world. Do you know why?"

"Tell me," I ask, pretending to be so sophisticated by rolling my eyes.

"Because…I get to see what's underneath the dress,"

he replies as his hand goes around to my back and gently pulls the zipper all the way down, letting the dress fall to the floor. "You are stunning, Appleton," he growls fiercely.

I feel a lurching sensation in my chest, then his hands start gliding over my naked torso, cupping my breasts, and gently pinching my nipples, making me gasp. I've never wanted anyone so much in my life.

He scoops me up with ease and carries me, naked but for the smallest red thong in the world, to the bedroom. I let out a yelp when he throws me onto the huge bed. Petals fly everywhere. He takes off my shoes one by one, carefully undoing the tiny buckles and tossing them on the floor.

I lie there and look up at him in awe. Watching as he unbuttons his shirt and flings it away. My eyes feast on his toned and tanned beautiful body. There's nothing more that I want than to feel his naked flesh on mine.

I sit up and crawl towards him, our eye contact so intense I can't look away. Reaching for his pants, I unbuckle his belt, undo the top button, and very, very, very slowly pull the zipper down. I run my hands over his black briefs, his cock already beautifully hard.

Jackson groans low in his throat as I touch him.

Chapter Fifty-Five

JACKSON

"Lauren," I gasp. I can't even begin to describe the sensations this woman arouses in me. She truly can bring me to my knees with just a smile or a look from those soft eyes of her. I feel as if I belong to her heart and soul. As if I've always been waiting for her.

"You make me so damn hot, baby," I groan.

"Oh yeah," she replies throatily with a naughty expression in her eyes.

"What is it?"

She lays back on the bed. "Watch me," she purrs.

She opens her legs wide and I see the black string of her thong stuck between her pussy lips. I feel my breath hitch and my heart starts beating faster with excitement. Jesus! She playing the part of a dirty slut, but that black string stuck between her flesh, is the sweetest most innocent thing I've ever seen.

Licking her lips, she lifts the black string and exposes her glistening pink folds. She curls her hips upwards presenting all of her to me. Her face, her ripe breasts, her pussy, all of it was exposed to my eyes. I can even see the tightly puckered flesh of her ass. My balls tighten in anticipation. One day that will be mine too.

"Do it," I snarl. Who the hell am I? When she is around, I become an animal.

Her fingertips brush her clit lightly and her mouth opens in a moan of pleasure. Her fingers slide lower, caressing the lips of her pussy, sliding back and forth along either side. Then she slides her index finger inside, a furtive, almost shy dip. It is as if her pussy sucks in her whole finger. Her finger begins to slide back out, before darting back in as deep as it will go. As she fingers herself, her back arches. I watch hungrily as she slides two fingers into her pussy, plunging them in deep while her hips rock and her nipples stiffen with pleasure.

When she adds a third finger and pushes them all in. I cannot help my hand from fisting my cock and stroking myself.

"Do you want me to stop?" she asks, her voice throaty.

"No." I want to see it all. I watch her fingers plunging in and out faster and faster until her entire body stiffens and she starts to come.

Then I reach down and pull her hand away from her body so I can watch her pussy come in all its glorious exquisite detail: swollen, twitching, and spurting hot juices. Her cheeks are deliciously rosy and her body is still bowed when I crouch between her legs, desperate to taste and pleasure her. I lick her wet pussy. Her hands claw into my hair.

Loving the taste and the scent of her, I thrust my tongue deeper inside. Like a fat kid sucking ice cream I suck and lick her until another orgasm barrels through her body and her sweet cum spills into my mouth and runs down my chin.

"I want to ride you." Her voice is thick with desire.

I sit at the edge of the bed and watch her breasts bounce as she straddles me. Her hand slips around behind my neck and she begins to slowly ride me, as if on a bucking bronco, grinding her hips on me, her flat stomach rolling with each movement. Then she drags her open pussy along the entire length of my erection.

"Holy fuck!" I growl.

Her hand comes up to her breast, and her finger traces around her nipple, caressing it. Then she throws her head back and thrusts her chest forward. When I bend my head towards it, the little tease pulls away.

I groan with frustration.

The involuntary sound brings her nipple closer again.

This time I move faster, but she has already anticipated it, and all I manage to do is dart my tongue out and lick the bud before she moves out of reach. I start to positively ache for the taste of them. When her nipples come closer, fast as lightning, I suck one of the tight little pink nubs into my mouth.

My hand reaches for the condom, but she grabs my hand and stops me. "We won't need that. I want to feel your bare cock deep inside me." She pauses. "Please," she mouths silently.

I stare at her. God, I want nothing more.

Smiling softly, she raises her ass and curls her hand around my dick. Watching my face for my reaction, she positions herself over it and slowly, inch by inch, sits on the thick shaft of my cock. As her pussy is stretched and filled to its limit, she closes her eyes and moans softly as if she is experiencing something divine. Then she begins to ride me hard and firm, her pussy milking my cock. It sends me over the edge. Pleasure explodes inside me, I pump out spurt after spurt of my cum inside her.

Lauren then lays against my body, exhausted and satiated.

She doesn't say anything, but the tip of her tongue traces a love heart on my neck.

J ackson

"Making you smile is the best feeling in the world," I tell her as we sit on the balcony wrapped in fluffy white hotel bathrobes and having breakfast in the warm morning sun,

She grins. Even blushes a little.

"All of this is amazing," she says, looking around. "But you make me smile without any of this. Not that I'm complaining."

"I hope not. As this is the best French toast I've ever had!" I pop the last piece into my mouth and top up our coffee cups.

"With the best view," she adds, buttering a croissant.

"I still can't believe your friend Pam is David's fiancée! That's crazy."

"I know! I told the girls this morning and they couldn't believe it either. The wedding is going to be so much fun."

"And I get to go home with one of the bridesmaids. I always wanted to do that," I say, winking at her.

"There are three bridesmaids. I hope you mean me."

"Every other girl fades in comparison to you, Lauren," I state seriously

She rolls her eyes and gives me a look. "Clyde, I

thought you were meant to be a dangerous bad boy not a romantic sap."

I laugh. "Oh, really? Anymore talk like that and I'll have to take you back to bed and show you just how bad I can be."

Her eyes twinkle with naughtiness and my cock twitches under my robe. "Fine. You have no one to blame, but yourself."

She shrieks with giggles as I hoist her over my shoulder and carry her back to our messy bed, sheets and petals strewn everywhere. I throw her onto the bed, tugging her bathrobe open and bury my head between her sweet thighs.

Chapter Fifty-Six

LAUREN

I sigh with contentment as the masseuse wraps me in a towel and leaves us alone in the dimly lit room of the hotel spa, soothing music playing and scented candles burning. I look over at Jackson and he's smiling at me dopily.

"That was so good," I whisper.

He nods and stretches his arm out towards me.

I take his hand and smile to myself, thinking about our gorgeous lazy day. From our amazing breakfast with a view, making love and watching a horror movies, then finally an hour long massage to end the perfect day.

"It's been amazing," I whisper to him again. "Thank you for everything."

"My pleasure," he tells me. "But it's not over yet," he adds, winking and slowly pulling himself to his feet.

I ease myself up too, my body feeling supple and refreshed. "What do you mean?"

"You'll see," he says mysteriously. Once we're dressed though, he tells me that it's nothing special. "I just booked us a table for dinner, that's all."

He leads me through the hotel lobby to one of the restaurants and I gasp when we get inside. It's like a tropical paradise with a pool in the middle and a band playing on a gondola-style boat.

"Never been here before?"

I shake my head, looking around, taking it all in. "This place is cool."

Then, across the hazily-lit room, I notice a blonde bob... a head of long black curls... a brightly colored cap that can only belong to one person. I look up at Jackson in surprise but he's smiling.

"Shall we go and join them?" he says, his eyes full of love.

"Did you arrange this?" I ask him. Of course, he did. "You're something else," I say, shaking my head in amazement.

As we head towards them, I realize Pam is there too. Matthew as well, sitting next to Nina. And a tall dark gentleman in a suit next to Andrea who must be Ricardo!

"Hi everyone!" I yell as we reach the table.

"Hey lovebirds," Andrea grins, standing up to greet us.

Everyone else follows suit and I'm grinning from ear to ear. Now this really is the perfect end to a perfect weekend.

"So, how come you're not in Tahoe, Jackson?" Pam asks.

"Work commitments," he grunts.

I punch his arm. "Are you referring to me as work?"

He laughs, catches my hand, puts his arm around my waist possessively. It makes me wonder if this is for Mathews benefit. I should tell him I'm not Mathew's type, or maybe I won't. It's wonderful to be so wanted.

He addresses Pam, "Have you heard from them?"

"Nope," she says, rolling her eyes. "I don't think I want to know what they're up to, to be honest."

"I won't show you the photos Joe sent me then," Jackson says, smirking.

Pam's eyes grow wide.

He laughs and gets out his phone. "Relax. It's nothing to worry about." He shows us all a picture of a group of guys all dressed up in bear suits with their skis and poles, on top of a mountain.

"Oh, my God," she cries out laughing, "What the heck!"

"Aw, I bet you wish you were there," I say to him.

"Are you kidding? I've had the best weekend with you." He smiles at me, his green eyes twinkling.

I smile back so hard, it feels as if my face could break into two.

"You guys make me want to throw up!" Andrea cackles.

I give her a look.

"Andrea, have you not got a single romantic bone in your body?" Ricardo asks in a sexy Italian accent, but his dark eyes are smiling.

"I think you have enough romance in you for the both of us!" Andrea retorts.

I wonder what she means. She certainly hasn't told us about any of his romantic gestures and I make a note to grill her about it later.

We take our seats in the two empty spaces next to Nina and Matthew. I'm a little apprehensive to see how Jackson and Matthew will interact but to my relief, they shake each other's hands affably.

"How's it going, man?" Jackson says, grinning.

"Great, thanks." He's beaming and so is Nina sitting next to him.

I'm happy to see that my match-making skills seem to be working well so far!

"Thanks so much for taking Draco out today," I tell Nina. "And for all the photos! You took him for a long walk. I bet he's exhausted!"

"He wolfed down his food and then he's been sleeping on the sofa all afternoon," she reports.

"After he almost got his hands on my lunch!" Matthew chimes in. "He's a gorgeous dog you've got there. If a little greedy."

I'm laughing. "Oh god, I know. He'll eat anything that one! He has a particular penchant for pizzas!"

"And cupcakes," Jackson adds, grinning.

Nina bursts out laughing and Matthew glances at her for an explanation.

I give her a warning look. I'd rather I build up my reputation at work a little more before he finds out anything about the love potion saga. "How's the project going?" I ask Danny quickly.

"Wonderfully, thanks," he says, adjusting his cap. "Although I was a little late going in today… distractions…" he adds with a knowing look.

"Handyman Darren?" I ask.

His face tells me I'm right. I smile back happily.

Chapter Fifty-Seven

LAUREN

One Week Later.

"Draco, where are you?"

I hear the pad of his slow footsteps coming towards me from my bedroom and meet him in the hall, giving him a big hug. His tail is wagging furiously.

"Aw, I missed you too, sweetheart," I tell him, nuzzling my face into his scraggy fur.

Jackson's laughing at me. "It's only been two days without him, you soppy thing. I'll have to make sure I invite him for our next weekend away then, won't I?"

My eyes light up and I grin. "Next weekend away? That sounds nice. Where are we going?"

"Wherever you want, my gorgeous girl. I'd take you to the moon if I could!"

"Hmm not sure I'd even want to go to the moon to be honest," I say with a laugh.

"Well, how about Tahoe then? There's a few weeks left

of the season… and some great hiking around there too. I bet Draco would love it."

"That sounds amazing!" I tell him. "Maybe we could get somewhere with a hot tub? Andrea gave me a great tip I want to try out."

He grins. "Oh, really? You're getting tips from Andrea now, are you?

"Trust me, you'll like this one." My cheeks get hot just thinking about Andrea's tip.

He puts his hand on my face and I look up at him again. "Lauren… I know this might not be the most romantic setting to tell you this," he says, from his position on the floor of my hallway, sitting there cross-legged with Draco in between us.

"We can go sit on the couch?" I offer.

"No, wait," he says. "My heart is beating faster and faster."

I look at him, surprised by his admission. "Really?"

"Lauren… I love you. I love you so much. I love everything about you. Your tenderness. Your craziness. Your ambition. Your love for your friends, and your dear old dog. I think you're the most amazing woman I've ever met."

He's holding my hands. My heart feels like it's going to explode. Draco nudges me with his paw as if to say, go on, say something. And even the little cynical Andrea in my head is asking me what the hell I'm waiting for. Why I didn't say it before? Of course, there is nothing to be scared of. He's not going to hurt me. I can just come out and say it.

"I love you too," I blurt out.

Draco lets out a cheerful yap and we both start giggling then we're in each other's arms. Kissing each other like there's no tomorrow.

"So, no more silly arguments," he says.

I nod. "No more getting jealous of work colleagues," I add.

He grins and nods too.

My phone buzzes on the floor next to me and I glance at it. Then pick it up when I see the sender.

"Zelda?"

"Is that the gypsy?" he asks, curiously.

I nod and open the message warily.

All's well that ends well. True love comes to those who deserve it.

"That's so weird," I say. "How could she know?"

Jackson shrugs. "Don't ask me. I've never met the woman."

"Are you glad I went to her, Jackson?"

"Look, I know it's too early to talk about serious stuff," he whispers. "But one day, I'm going to ask you to marry me. I've never been so sure of anything in my life."

I try to laugh or act cool, but the tears start rolling down my cheeks. Then I'm shaking my head, saying sorry, laughing and crying at the same time.

He's laughing too and hugging me tight.

I just know everything is going to be ok. With or without the magic cupcake!

The End

Cherry Popper

(SAMPLE CHAPTERS)

Chapter One

Mia

My head knew, and maybe my heart always knew, but my body stood there like a damn fool.

Shocked to see the two of them like this. Going at it like *wild* animals! The world outside ground to a screeching halt. I stared at them in astonishment. Really, Mark? You picked Bella. Of all our friends, you choose her, the girl you insisted more than once had less sex appeal than a park bench on a Monday afternoon.

Less than five minutes ago, I had walked in through the front door of our apartment, a big cake precariously balanced on the palm of my left hand, so I could reach for my keys. A big-ass smile was plastered all over my face because I was really pleased with myself.

I had to travel all the way across town to a specialist bakery to find the perfect cake for the surprise birthday party I was throwing for Mark that evening, but I just knew he would adore the red velvet and butter cream treat I chose. True, as a rule he didn't eat junk food. I should know, it'd been months since we ordered in pizza and just kicked back to enjoy ourselves, but surely, even he would allow himself to have a slice, or maybe even two of this delicious dream of a concoction.

My plan was to drop the cake off before heading out to pick up the booze I'd ordered. My intention was to have it free-flowing all evening long. Usually, with alcohol in his system, Mark loosened up, and hopefully we could have some fun times later in the night. Not that I was saying we never had sex anymore without the help of lots of alcohol, or that he wasn't fun. It was not really his fault he'd been so uptight. He had a very stressful job. If I had a job like his I would be murder to deal with too. His boss was a real psychopath.

I had just got the door open when I heard the noise. It sounded like a grunt. What a pig or a wild boar would make.

I froze on the spot. What the hell would a pig or wild boar be doing in my apartment? My head whirled around as my ears zeroed in on the location of the sound. It took me a good few seconds to figure out where it was coming from. I located the place where the sounds had come from just as my eyes fell onto a trail of clothes on the floor, one that led a messy path to the bedroom.

An idiot could have figured out the scene, but at that moment, my pride simply refused to believe it. It couldn't be. I mean, this scenario was just so cliché. Something you saw in movies, for God's sake.

I put the cake down carefully on the table as I'd put a lot of effort into getting it. Then I followed the clothes.

A scarf: Hmm…

A tie: Okay. But still not conclusive. Not really.

A shirt I purchased for him a couple of Christmases ago: Well, it was summer and it was hot. Very hot. Even I was in a tank top.

A pair of slutty leopard print thongs with white slime on the crotch string: Ugh…Oh God!

The penny finally dropped, but to be honest I felt surprisingly calm in the face of what was happening. Maybe because none of it seemed real. I wasn't meant to be back here, and some part of me felt as if I wasn't. Like I was drifting in and watching someone else sneaking around our apartment. The sounds got louder even as the carpet muted my footsteps.

I arrived at our bedroom door and stopped in my tracks.

Chapter Two

Mia

He was behind Bella, fucking her roughly, hands grabbing her skinny hips. His back was to me, but in the dressing table mirror, I could see his face. It looked so red and contorted it was hard to tell whether it was pleasure or pain he was experiencing. Neither could see me and oblivious to my presence they carried on groaning, grunting, and emitting guttural cries of encouragement to each other. You know, stuff like, faster, harder, yeah baby, so good, etc.

I knew I should shout, or draw attention to myself and let them know I had caught them in the act. Here was my fiancé, balls-deep in one of *our* friends, in the middle of the day, in the middle of the apartment that I paid half for. It should have made me incredulous, but in fact, it made perfect sense. Now that I really looked back on it, it seemed so obvious.

Bella, who always said, I should ditch Mark, because he was such a dork. Mark who always said, Bella was so sexless, if she were a man she would have been a eunuch. Eunuch, my ass. She was wriggling her sweat-soaked body like a damn snake in an effort to get more of him inside her. Granted, there wasn't that much to get inside, but even so. What a slut! I tilted my head slightly and looked at his dick. Thank God, for small mercies. He was wearing a condom.

I stood there for what seemed like a lifetime, blankly watching them go at it and thinking of my next move. I thought about saying something. Well, okay, screaming something, but it seemed undignified. I would have to yell louder than them. No, I wouldn't do that. I should let them get on with it. I was better off without them.

I turned and headed back out to the front door. I could still see them in the act, an image that was going to be burned onto my brain for the rest of my life, but that was okay. I could live with it. I'd seen worse on TV, on Animal Planet.

As I was passing through the living room I glanced at the cake on the table, and felt the sudden urge to slam my hand down on it, to send the frosting and the perfectly-defined layers squishing messily out all over the table, but I restrained myself. No, I had put a lot of effort into getting it and I wasn't wasting it. I picked up the cake and went back to the bedroom.

They were still going at it.

Unbelievable! Pigs!

I walked right up to Mark. The bastard never broke the stride of his thrusts or noticed me. With all my strength, I smashed the dream cake over his head.

His reaction was freaking priceless. He was so startled, he fell forward with a girlish scream. Right on top of Bella, the slut, trapping her underneath him. Her thin limbs flailed around like those of a giant insect.

I looked down at my handiwork with satisfaction.

The cake didn't just break into a few pieces, there was cake and cream everywhere. On their naked bodies, the bed, the carpet. The mess was incredible. Both were still reeling with shock and had no idea what had hit them when I turned around smartly and walked out of the bedroom. I could hear him swearing and her shouting as I marched out of the apartment. I didn't even bother to close the front door.

A smile cracked out over my face. To my surprise, it turned into a mad little giggle. I guess, because:

1. They looked absolutely ridiculous.
2. There would be consequences, but for now, I was glad I broke up their sex session in such a spectacular fashion.
3. Mark had just handed me my Get Out Of Jail Free card.

Still giggling to myself, I made my way back to my car. I had almost reached my car when the bedroom window of our apartment was thrown open and Mark called out to me. At first, he sounded quite desperate as he begged me to come back up and talk to him. Then to my disbelief and fury, he had the nerve to shout down that it was not what I thought it was. It was all a big misunderstanding.

Un-freaking-believable. I couldn't help feeling a bit curious about how he planned to spin the fact that I had seen his dick inside her. But was I going back up there and let him lie to my face? No chance. No way. I didn't want to see either of them ever again.

Quite frankly, Bella was more than welcome to him.

Let her put up with his prissy ways. Instead of feeling hurt, like I knew I should, I experienced only a sense of relief. It was weird, but I felt as though a weight I'd been carrying since the day he popped the question had been lifted at last. Gratitude to the universe for showing me the truth bloomed, like fragrant petals, inside my heart. Sunshine beamed down at me.

I gazed up at bright blue sky and felt good.

I didn't have to feel bad about walking away from such a 'great catch' or defend my decision to anyone. There wasn't a thing anyone could say. Not a damn thing. Anyway, there wasn't a person alive who could have argued that I should stick by him. Not even my mother would be able to act as if this was my fault for being too fussy, or choosy.

I had escaped him—that fucker, the man who came so close to being my husband. I realized now it would have been a fate worse than death. The only real quality I appreciated and valued in him was his loyalty and he had just flushed that down a toilet called Bella.

A flash of burning fury sped through my body as I thought of all the trouble I had taken to set up his party.

Bastard.

Asshole.

Piece of shit.

I climbed into the driver's seat. Yes, he was a jerk, yes, I wasted a year of my life, but hey, I was free now! I was finally FREE! For the first time in years, I felt completely and utterly liberated. I clamped my hands over the wheel, and turned my head to look in his direction. He was still hanging out of the window covered in his cake and begging me to come back. My anger disappeared and a bubble of laughter burst out of my mouth.

He stopped begging and stared at me with open-mouthed astonishment.

Yeah, put that in your pipe and smoke it.

I pulled out of the parking lot as I left him, her, and our life together behind. This was it for me. I drove around for a little while, not quite sure where precisely I was going, but without meaning to, I found myself heading toward the outskirts of the city.

Julie's wedding. Back in Cold Creek.

I was supposed to be leaving tomorrow after work with Mark, but slight change of plans. That's where I was headed now on my own. Only a couple of hours away, back home, and far removed from this entire mess and everything that came with it.

All I had in the back was my purse, one packed bag for the trip, and a dry-cleaning token, but that didn't matter. What mattered was: I was free again to restart my life and this time, I wasn't settling for second best.

Never again!

Chapter Three

Mia

I remembered the first time we met. Two years ago, when I'd been dragged along by my friend, Irene to some top-level fundraiser. Even though she'd warned me it would be boring, and I'd only gone out of solidarity, I'd been seriously regretting my decision. So, when some halfway cute finance bro started hitting on me, I decided I might as well just go along with it for fun.

I expected it to be a very short romance. My reaction to finding him inside our friend is proof if I ever needed it... that I was never really into him. What happened was my mother basically slammed the accelerator on our relationship when she found out about his family and his job. I just went along with it because I had nothing better in my life. All my friends had boyfriends and husbands, so to be honest, it seemed more worthwhile cooking for two than one. Plus, I liked the idea of having someone to take me to parties and bring me home afterward. The sex was never all that. He seemed to be having way more fun with Bella. Which, I had to admit hurt far more than his deception.

Hmmm….was it me? Was I no good at sex?

When he proposed, I remember hesitating for a split second. The part of me which I did my best to clamp down on, reared its head. It howled at me to stop and think about what I was getting myself into. Then, I saw the ring glinting in its box, his face full of anticipation, the whole restaurant holding its breath as everyone waited for my reply.

A million thoughts raced through my head.

He really shouldn't have asked me in such a public place. It limited my responses. An answer like 'maybe in the future' would have been fine in our living room, bit it was out of the question in front of that hopeful audience. Obviously, if I said no, I would be back at square one. No boyfriend. I could hear my mother saying, *"I can't believe you let a good man like that go. What on earth are you waiting for? A prince on a white horse?"*

To spare them all the embarrassment, I agreed.

People came up to congratulate us and I started to think I had made the right decision. Not everybody can fall head over heels with someone. Some people, people like me, had to compromise and settle for less. Well, not less exactly. Mark was definitely a catch, but he was also the practical choice. Yes, I gave up on fantasy and made the right choice.

Then, before I knew it, I found myself lost in planning for the big society wedding that my mother wanted. But at night, alone, when he was out of town, I would doubt the man I was getting married to. Then, I'd find myself searching for ways out, but have you ever tried to cut off a marriage when things were already in motion?

I was scared shitless about the money, time, and effort everyone had wasted on my behalf. I just couldn't be the bitch who let everyone down. I could already envision the sadness on my dad's face along with the disappointment and censure on my mom's. So I would get out of bed, gulp down a very large glass of wine, and tell myself I was one of the lucky ones. I had a good man. A man who loved me. A man who wanted to marry me and take care of me. He'd even begun to build a house for us. I'd be an ungrateful fool if I ever gave him up.

I would fall asleep telling myself over and over again, that I'd made the right decision.

But now, that the good man had cheated on me...with one of my friends, well, ex-friends, I had a get out of jail card. And I intended to use it.

I drove and drove, my brain racing, memories flooding my head, until I realized my stomach was growling. There was a diner up the road and I decided to pull over. I'd always loved the idea of stopping for waffles and maybe a milkshake at crappy roadside diners to break up the trip, but whenever I took Mark back to my hometown, he would always insist that we wait until we were at my parents' place before we ate.

Guess what? He wasn't here to stop me.

I could do whatever the hell I wanted!

I pulled the car over, looked at myself in the mirror, and tried to connect with my reflection. I reminded myself that I was her, this woman who had just dumped her fiancé, and cut town without so much as a glance back. I grinned and winked at her. She grinned and winked back at me. I was on a roll. I reached for my phone.

I took a while drafting the text, wanting to wring as much of my vitriol out on to him as I could. I hovered my fingers over the keys, thinking about all the ways I could tear him a new one. I wanted his stomach to drop out of his ass when he got this text, as it sunk into him just how little he had hurt me, and that required the perfect balance of anger, superiority, and a bye-bitch-titude. I spent a while crafting the perfect message, then I sat back and read it one more time before I hit send.

Hey Dick Head,

Since I just walked in on you fucking Bella, I just wanted to let you know the wedding's off. Hope you had a good time. Apartment's all yours. Rent is paid until the end of the month so I'll come around and pick up my stuff before then. Oh, also I planned a surprise birthday party for you tonight. Booze has been ordered from Hall and Greek, but hasn't been paid for yet. Please pick it up before 5pm and get back to the apartment before 8pm. Tip: might be a good idea to act surprised because your boss will be there too. Good luck with explaining to all our friends why I'm not there.

I hit send and leaned back. Closing my eyes, I let the air escape from my lungs slowly. Wow, but it felt good to hit him with that. There it was… code red, my whole life blown up over the course of one message. There was no way I could go back now, and I was fine with that.

Fuck him.

Fuck Bella.

Fuck me for ever thinking I should have stuck it out with him.

A knock on my window jerked me out of my internal world. I opened my eyes and a man was asking me if I was all right. I pulled the biggest grin my face would stretch to and gave him the thumbs up sign.

He smiled back, nodded and walked away.

Right. Time to start over. First things first. I blocked Mark's number. Then I got out of the car and stretched. The bright sun beamed down on me as I walked to the diner. I felt strangely light and free. Inside, I ordered waffles and a milkshake; then got a piece of pie to finish up.

If Mark had been here, he would have been pulling faces about me gaining weight, about not wanting a fat bride to walk down the aisle, but he could blow me. I was eating all the damn pie I wanted, because I wasn't going to be a fat bride. I wasn't going to be *any* kind of bride.

I thought back to the dresses, to all the outfits I had tried on in the hopes that I would find something that didn't feel completely wrong for me. Now, looking back it was so obvious that the problem was the man, not the dress. Nothing felt right because *he* wasn't right. But now he was gone, and I had a feeling everything was going to make a lot more sense.

I still had a few questions, of course. How long had it been going on? How many times had Bella looked me in the eye and laughed uproariously at my jokes as if it was the funniest thing she'd ever heard in her whole life while she was fucking my fiancé behind my back?

But right now, I felt happy just letting those niggling issues go unanswered and concentrated on how I would handle the backlash; the questions from my family about what had happened. I was going to be blunt as hell and hope that got the point across. "Sorry that I wasted your time and money, but I'm not going to marry the man I caught in bed with one of our friends."

Damn, my mother would go *crazy* when she found out.

I finished up my food and got back in the car. It was such a beautiful day, I put the convertible top down and turned on the radio. Bruce Springsteen's raspy voice filled the air. *Born in the USA* was one of my old favorites so I turned the volume up to the maximum. It'd been a long time since I'd done this. I bounced in my seat while singing along with Springsteen as I hit the highway. Life was for living and that was exactly what I intended to do.

Some people might have been nervous, heading to one of their most competitive friend's wedding straight after they called off their own, but I felt no such worries. It felt like something had been set on fire within me. A cleansing flame, one that burned out everything which had been bringing me down all this time. I focused on the wind blowing through my hair and let the rays of the sun filter through the trees either side of me and warm my skin, as a smile spread across my face once more. Yes, this was good. Great. Perfect, just—

And that's when the car spluttered, started to cough and slow down.

Chapter Four

Mia

"Oh shit," I muttered and quickly pulled to the side of the road. I climbed out to see what was wrong. I walked all around it. No smoke or anything serious. No burning smell. The tires were all okay. As a matter of fact, I couldn't see anything immediate, but when I got back in and tried to kick it into gear, it let out a wet flub of a noise and died again.

Fuck.

I got out once more and peered both ways down the road. The road was empty and I hadn't seen any cars for at least half-an-hour. I was still a couple of miles out of town. I'd hoped to make my triumphant re-entrance under my own steam, but it became obvious it was going to be one of those days. Disasters come in threes. I caught my husband-to-be cheating on me and now I would have to call my parents to help me. I wonder what the third one would be? Still, being stranded like this sucked.

I'd been hoping for a dignified conversation at my family's home of why Mark wasn't with me, but I supposed dropping the news on my mother in the back of the car on the way back home with a cheerful look on my face would have just as much impact as pulling up in my own car alone.

I dialed their number, leaned against the car, and enjoyed the quiet before the tone started to buzz in my ear. Once, twice, three times, and then it went to messages.

"We're out at a luncheon right now, but please feel free to leave a message and we'll call back later," my mother's cultured voice cooed down the line.

Damn! How many times had I told her she didn't need to change their message every single time they left the house? She just wanted everyone to know what high-society bullshit they were up to at all times. So, they were out and if they were at lunch, that meant they were going to be a while. So where did that leave me?

I sighed and dumped my phone back in the car. The buzz from everything that had happened today was beginning to fade, and I found myself getting seriously annoyed. Would I just have to walk the rest of the way into town? I peered down at my shoes. They were three inches high and definitely not meant for walking. I was a good couple of miles out right now, and I had zero intention of turning my feet into blistering red sores.

I frowned. I supposed I could call one of my old friends. I tried Shana. While she sounded excited to hear from me, she couldn't come because she was at the hair-dressers. She suggested calling her cousin, but I had never kept in touch with her and I didn't want to ask her for help.

I stood there wondering if I should call the bride, when it clicked.

I remembered that there was a garage not far from where I was. Sure, it would still be a good half-hour walk, but maybe it would do me good to work off some of the excess energy pulsing around my system since I'd left the city. I was pretty sure the place was still open. At least, it was when Mark and I passed it a month ago. Even if it wasn't, I might be able to flag someone down from there, or get the number of a reliable tow truck company.

I started on the walk down to the garage, loading up some music on my phone to listen to as I strolled. The air felt dry and hot, but clean. I liked the sensation of having flat countryside on either side of me. This was my home. The place I couldn't wait to get out of at one time in my life. Yet, now since I was older and wiser, I could appreciate it for what it was. It was real.

I thought of my crummy job in the city. I'd given my blood, sweat and tears for it and yet, I could be replaced as easily as a lightbulb. Maybe I should move back out here, start a rescue service for women who had their cars break down in the middle of nowhere. This place clearly needed it.

Finally, I rounded a bend and spotted the garage I'd seen before. I plucked my earbuds out of my ears and stared at the building. It looked so beat-up that for a moment I thought it was closed, but then I heard some male voices coming from the main building and realized there were people inside. I hurried toward it, switching off my music, and patting my hair into place. I wasn't sure why, but I felt a strange little flutter in my chest.

Maybe nerves. Maybe something else entirely.

A man passed me as I got close. I opened my mouth to greet him and ask for help, but he dropped his head and made his way straight to his car, pulling down onto the road and leaving me standing there like an idiot. I raised my eyebrows and shook my head. It might be easy to idealize this place when I'd been away as long as I had. But I did forget it was still the same slightly suspicious small town I had grown up in. I made my way toward the main building, where I could hear the sound of metalwork and a fuzzy old radio.

"Hello?" I called as I stepped inside and glanced around. It took me a moment to spot him, but I felt a wave of relief when I saw that I wasn't babbling to myself.

"Hi, hello." I ran my fingers through my hair and strode toward the pair of legs clad in oil-stained jeans sticking out from under an old, rusted car.

"Give me a second," a deep gravelly voice floated out from under the car, but made no move to show himself. I thought I recognized the voice but I couldn't place it straight off; I likely knew everyone in this town, anyway, so it wasn't a surprise that I would.

I stood there, arms crossed, tapping my foot impatiently as I counted to ten. Rude country hick! As if I hadn't been insulted enough by the male species for one damn day.

Finally, when I was just about to kick him hard, he pushed himself out from beneath the car, and—Jesus Christ.

Read more at….
Cherry Popper

Also by River Laurent

Come Say Hello!

Thank you so much for reading!
Join my Newsletter
Or
come and say hello on Facebook!

www.facebook.com/River-Laurent-1805481599711127

18704120R00166

Printed in Great Britain
by Amazon